Praise for *The Judge Who Stole Christmas* and other novels by Randy Singer

"A fresh approach to Christmas inspiration."
PUBLISHERS WEEKLY

"A seasonal winner—don't miss it!"
FAITHFULREADER.COM

"*The Judge Who Stole Christmas* is creative, relevant, well written, and highly entertaining, with engaging characters who are real and original but who ring with a familiarity that will capture your heart in an unexpected way."
RENE GUTTERIDGE
Author of *Listen* and the Boo series

". . . A book that will entertain readers and make them think—what more can one ask?"
PUBLISHERS WEEKLY
On *The Justice Game*

"Singer artfully crafts a novel that is the perfect mix of faith and suspense. . . . [*The Justice Game* is] fast-paced from the start to the surprising conclusion."
ROMANTIC TIMES

"At the center of the heart-pounding action are the moral dilemmas that have become Singer's stock-in-trade. . . . An exciting thriller."
BOOKLIST
On *By Reason of Insanity*

D0067396

the

JUDGE WHO STOLE CHRISTMAS

the

judge who stole
CHRISTMAS

RANDY SINGER

Tyndale House Publishers, Inc.
Carol Stream, Illinois

Visit Tyndale's exciting Web site at www.tyndale.com.

Visit Randy Singer's Web site at www.randysinger.net.

TYNDALE and Tyndale's quill logo are registered trademarks of Tyndale House Publishers, Inc.

The Judge Who Stole Christmas

Copyright © 2005 by Randy Singer. All rights reserved.

First printing by Tyndale House Publishers, Inc., in 2010.

Previously published as *The Judge Who Stole Christmas* by WaterBrook Press under ISBN: 1-4000-7057-0.

Cover photograph by Dan Farrell copyright © Tyndale House Publishers, Inc. All rights reserved.

Back cover and title page photographs by Jason Miller copyright © Tyndale House Publishers, Inc. All rights reserved.

Designed by Jessie McGrath

Published in association with the literary agency of Alive Communications, Inc., 7680 Goddard Street, Suite 200, Colorado Springs, CO 80920, www.alivecommunications.com.

Scripture taken from the New King James Version.® Copyright © 1982 by Thomas Nelson, Inc. Used by permission. All rights reserved.

Library of Congress Cataloging-in-Publication Data

Singer, Randy (Randy D.)
The judge who stole Christmas / Randy Singer.
   p. cm.
Originally published: Colorado Springs, Colo. : WaterBrook Press, 2005.
ISBN 978-1-4143-3566-7 (sc)
1. Judges—Fiction. 2. Church and state—Fiction. 3. Christmas stories. I. Title.
PS3619.I5725J83 2010
813′.6—dc22   2010018848

Printed in the United States of America

16 15 14 13 12 11 10
 7   6   5   4   3   2

This book is dedicated to the Christ child.

★

It's not as majestic as gold or frankincense or myrrh, but it's the best that I could do.

1

"Doggone it," Thomas grunted, glancing toward the Holstein as the big fella lifted its tail. "What're they feedin' that thing anyway?"

Theresa smiled to herself and watched the cow pie form on the wood chips blanketing the ground of their makeshift manger. Thomas shook his head, then hustled behind the partition that formed the back of their little stall, strategically located on one side of the Possum town square. He returned with a shovel and black plastic bag, scooping up the mess before a family of four climbed out of the Ford Explorer at the edge of the square. Visitors had been sparse tonight, kept away by a cold and steady drizzle. Plus, people didn't usually have time to visit the live manger scene this early in the season. There was simply too much shopping to do.

"I'd help you out, but I just got baby Jesus to sleep." Theresa cuddled the plastic doll wrapped in swaddling Walmart blankets. "You know what a momma's boy He is."

"Don't be disrespectful," Thomas muttered, his voice low so he couldn't be heard by the approaching family. They had learned that it somehow broke the reverence of the occasion if Mary and Joseph were bickering.

"Didn't mean no disrespect," Theresa whispered. She looked lovingly at the baby in her arms, its chubby little face glistening as the spotlight bounced off its plastic cheeks. It was only a doll, but it was special in so many ways. For two years this doll had played the part of the Christ child in the otherwise-live Nativity scene. And Theresa, who had been honored to take her shift as a thirty-five-year-old replica of the teenage Virgin Mary, had seen some pretty amazing things happen when people came to visit.

But the baby doll was special for other reasons as well. It was, after all, the favorite doll of Theresa's eight-year-old daughter, Hannah, a constant companion that Hannah had named "Bebo" when Hannah was only three. Bebo's plastic face, hands, and feet—once a clean and fleshy pink—now took on the hue of a Middle Eastern baby, colored by thousands of hugs, kisses, and strokes from Hannah's grubby little hands and lips. Bebo's cloth body had been patched twice in an effort to keep the stuffing from falling out. Other dolls and stuffed animals had come and gone in the Hammond household, but Bebo stayed around, sleeping under Hannah's arm every night.

Because she was nearly human anyway, Bebo was a

natural choice to play the Christ child. Nobody outside the Hammond family needed to know that Bebo was really a girl.

"What smells?" the approaching teenage girl asked as she turned up her nose and huddled under an umbrella with her mother.

"Maybe one of the shepherds let one rip," her younger brother said.

Theresa noticed Thomas stiffen, but she knew he would hold his tongue. As soon as the family left, however, Thomas would complain about the lack of discipline in families these days.

"Justin!" the boy's father snapped. He stood to the boy's side, hunched down in his own trench coat, seeking protection from the wind and drizzle.

"That's not even funny," the girl said.

"'That's not even funny,'" Justin mocked. "You're such a suck-up."

Theresa watched as the dad glared at Justin, but the boy avoided his father's eyes. She gauged Justin to be junior high age—thirteen, maybe fourteen. He was listening to his iPod, swaying slightly to its beat, his face shielded by a large hooded sweatshirt. Theresa thought about her own son, a little six-year-old pistol they had nicknamed Tiger. She wondered if she would survive Tiger as a teen.

"Amazing, isn't it?" the mother said as she stepped closer to Theresa and looked down at the Christ child. "That God loved us enough to send His Son to be born in a place like this."

Theresa nodded, flashing back to the delivery of her surprise baby—Elizabeth Leigh—ten months ago. The labor was brutal. But Mary—she delivered Jesus in a barn with Joseph as a midwife and with no epidurals.

"Amazing," Theresa muttered in agreement.

"It's not like He was born in Possum," Justin said.

But the mother ignored him and inched a little closer. After locking eyes with Theresa, she touched her fingers to her lips, kissed them, then placed them on the cheek of baby Jesus. Her daughter, without saying a word, did the same.

"Thanks for being out here, even in the rain," the mom said.

Theresa smiled and nodded. "God bless you," she said. She watched as the mom and her daughter locked arms under their umbrella, then turned and headed back to the car. As Justin trailed behind them, the dad began to follow but hesitated and turned back toward Theresa. He took a few tentative steps, looked deep into her eyes, and did something that always gave Theresa goose bumps.

He went down on one knee in front of her and bowed his head. She wanted to tell him to get up. The grass was wet and the Lord knew that nobody should be bowing to her. But the Lord also knew that this man didn't take a knee out of respect for some thirty-five-year-old mom who lived in a double-wide trailer in Possum. He was bowing before the Christ child, and Theresa had no right to interfere with that. She realized that Mary, the mother of Jesus, must have felt the same sense of unworthiness and awe when the shepherds came to honor her child.

She glanced at Thomas and saw the look of appreciation in his dark brown eyes. His face was shining, wet from the drizzle, and she could see fatigue in every muscle, but the look reflected her own thoughts—*This is why we're out here.*

After a few seconds, the man crossed himself and rose. He reached out and touched Theresa's hand even as she held tight to the make-believe baby. He squeezed softly. "Thanks," he said. Then he turned and walked away.

2

WITHIN AN HOUR the rain stopped and traffic picked up. Since Possum was a small town, Theresa recognized most of the folks, though there were always visitors she'd never seen before. She loved the children most. They would tentatively reach out to touch the dirty wool of the sheep, then jump back if the animals moved. Theresa would kneel down with the baby Jesus and watch the eyes of the kids light up as they took in the wonder of the Christ child. There were no lines for the live manger scene, never had been. But there would be a steady trickle—a family here, a couple there, a mom dragging along her kids and some friends a few minutes later.

This night Theresa was especially moved by a single mom who hauled three children, all under the age of five, to the manger. Though Theresa didn't recognize her, the woman confided in Theresa while Thomas occupied the kids with his mini herd of sheep and goats. The woman's husband left her not quite a year ago, just two days after Christmas, she told Theresa. She felt overwhelmed, trying to make it as a single mom, totally inadequate. Theresa reminded her that the Virgin Mary might have been a single mom when she raised the Son of God. We never hear from Joseph after that episode where they left Jesus at the temple as a very young boy, Theresa reasoned. God probably trusted the most important job in the world to a single mom. When they knelt and prayed, the woman couldn't hold back the tears.

A few minutes before ten, an earnest-looking man approached from the edge of the square.

Theresa guessed the stranger was in his early forties and probably had a fair amount of money. For one thing, he pulled up in a silver Mercedes-Benz, one of those diesel-engine cars that always sounded like it needed a tune-up. He had an impressive long, brown overcoat, a shiny gold watch, and a full head of slick black hair that probably required a stylist. He was a pretty boy as far as Theresa was concerned, medium height and thin, with a face you might find at a news anchor's desk, accessorized by a pair of round wire-rim glasses and a small stud earring in his left ear.

"You come out here every night?" the stranger asked. Theresa noticed the official-looking papers in his right hand.

Thomas looked him over before answering. "Not every night. We take turns with some others. We're out here Tuesdays and Thursdays."

The man nodded. "Even when it rains, huh?"

"Yep."

"You must believe pretty strongly in this."

"We do."

"You ever get a chance to minister to people spiritually?"

Though the man didn't raise his voice, Theresa could sense that Thomas resented the questions. Her husband, a big man with an enormous heart and a proven stubborn streak, planted his feet shoulder-width apart. His left hand held a shepherd's crook; his right hand was on his hip.

"Occasionally."

"I would guess you try to tell them about how the Christ child of Christmas can help meet their needs today."

"We try."

Theresa studied the differences between the two. Thomas, a beefy six-foot-two-inch former wrestler, made the stranger seem small. And Thomas certainly looked the part of a first-century craftsman with big, strong hands and a face leathered by outdoor work, his large frame wrapped in the robes of a biblical Israelite. But the stranger had a certain composure, even a haughtiness, that was making Theresa nervous. She suspected this would not end well.

"How do you think that makes others feel who are not Christians?" the man asked. "Jews, Muslims, atheists?"

Thomas looked a little incredulous at the question. "In Possum?" he asked.

"You don't think people like that ought to be welcome in Possum?" This time there was an edge to the man's voice.

"Welcome, sure," Thomas said. He glanced at Theresa and Bebo, then back at the stranger. "I wouldn't want them to be treated like Jesus was when He came to earth."

"Mmph," the man said. "Good." He, too, glanced at

Theresa, then returned a hardened gaze to Thomas. "Then maybe you'll understand what I've got to do." He handed a sheaf of documents to Thomas. "This is a lawsuit and subpoena for a court appearance on Monday in Norfolk federal court. I'm a lawyer for the ACLU, and what you're doing out here violates the separation of church and state."

Theresa saw the veins in Thomas's neck pulse. *Don't do anything stupid.* She took a few steps toward him to put a reassuring hand on his arm.

"The town asked us to do this." Thomas's eyes had the steely edge that Theresa had seen before. "See that tree over there?" The stranger didn't turn. "The town attorney said we'd be okay as long as we have that Christmas tree and Santa's sleigh over there." Thomas pointed to another corner of the square that hosted a replica of the jolly elf's transportation, though Santa himself never bothered to show up until the weekend before Christmas.

The ACLU lawyer didn't seem impressed. "The town attorney is wrong," he said. "Under the First Amendment, an empty sleigh and a pine tree with a few Christmas ornaments doesn't justify what you're doing."

"Well," Thomas replied, "I don't know about all that, but I ain't leavin' . . ."

Theresa tugged on his arm a little. "Thomas, it's okay—"

"*No*, it's *not* okay, Theresa." Thomas stood to his full height. "We're not going to let some ACLU lawyer waltz in here and just shut us down. Not on my watch."

"Why don't we let the courts decide that, shall we?" The lawyer's condescending tone made even Theresa a little angry, but her main focus right now was keeping Thomas calm. "You understand you've been served with a court document?" the lawyer asked, as if Thomas were a two-year-old. "It requires you to appear Monday along with representatives from the town that I'll also subpoena. I'll be calling you to testify."

Thomas didn't answer, but Theresa felt the muscles tighten on his forearm.

"You read that okay?" the lawyer asked, tilting his head a little to the side. "You understand the importance of that?"

"Oh yeah," Thomas said, looking down at the document as if the devil himself had subpoenaed him to appear in hell. "I guarantee ya, I'll treat it with all the respect it's due."

"As you should," the attorney said.

Without another word, Thomas turned and walked behind the partition, returning with a black garbage bag in his left hand. While the lawyer watched, Thomas walked over to his little entourage of sheep, used the subpoena to scoop up the sheep droppings, then threw the papers and the pellets in the trash.

He walked back to face the lawyer. "Thanks for coming by," Thomas said.

"I'll see you in court," the lawyer said.

"You sure will," Thomas replied.

The lawyer stared for a moment, then turned and walked away.

Theresa, now standing a few feet away, looked down at the baby in her arms. *Please, Jesus,* she prayed, *not again.*

3

FRIDAY, DECEMBER 1

"Jazz Woodfaulk!"

Jasmine cringed. She had been trying to get rid of that nickname since her glory days on the hardwood. Good lawyers didn't need cool nicknames. But Pearson Payne—First Amendment legend and partner in Gold, Franks & Mearns, one of New York City's most-storied law firms—could call her anything he wanted. He made no effort to hide his enthusiasm as he rose from behind his polished mahogany desk and bounded halfway across his huge corner office. He pumped Jasmine's hand and nodded dismissively at Andre, the young associate who had escorted Jasmine from one partner's office to another all morning.

"Old Dominion versus Tennessee, 2001 finals." Payne smiled as he recalled the moment. "Who was that point guard of yours—missed that baseline jumper with just a few seconds left?"

"Maya," Jasmine answered.

"Yeah, Maya." Payne let go of the hand but stayed uncomfortably close, his light blue eyes dancing. "I'll never forget that put-back of yours at the buzzer."

Jasmine gave the man a quizzical look. "We still lost by five," she said.

"Yeah, but the spread in Vegas was six," Payne shot back. "Your shot put ten thousand bucks into my grandkids' college fund."

Jasmine resisted a smile. She immediately liked this guy, though he seemed more like an old gym rat than a distinguished partner in a big New York firm.

"Six points," Payne continued, shaking his head at the absurdity of it. "Tennessee might have had Pat Summitt stalking the sidelines, but ODU had Jazz Woodfaulk on the court!"

He patted the outside of her arm, and Jasmine was starting to get a little embarrassed by this stroll down memory lane. The 2001 NCAA Finals, though her team had lost, was still the pinnacle of an up-and-down basketball career that ended a year later with her third knee injury—a torn ACL. Jasmine was now in her third year of law school, and basketball seemed like a whole other life. Though she loved Pearson Payne's enthusiasm, she wanted to be taken seriously as a prospective lawyer, not as a former hoops star.

"Have a seat," Payne said.

"Thanks." Jasmine settled her six-two frame into one

of the brown leather chairs in front of Payne's desk. She smoothed her black pin-striped skirt and crossed her legs. Payne slid onto the front of the desk, one leg on the floor, the other dangling off the desk. He was every bit as tall as Jasmine—maybe an inch or two taller—rail-thin and full of explosive energy. He wore suspenders and a red bow tie, accentuating his reputation as a free spirit in a place that valued conformity. Though Jasmine knew Payne was fifty-five years old, she would never have guessed it. He had a perfect head of gray hair, an impressive tan for the first week of December, and the sharp facial lines of a much younger man. *Do senior partners in New York law firms get face-lifts?* Jasmine wondered.

"How's the knee?" he asked.

"It feels great," Jasmine said. She wanted to turn the conversation away from old basketball injuries to the issue at hand—a job offer. "Once those old cadaver ligaments got used to hauling my frame around, I started feeling great."

Payne glanced at the knee and smiled. "The bionic woman."

"Not hardly," Jasmine replied. The knee had kept her from going pro, and they both knew it.

Payne grabbed Jasmine's résumé from his desk—finally—and perused it while Jasmine felt her palms start to sweat. She was sitting in front of the chief outside legal counsel for the *New York Times*. He had argued in front of the U.S. Supreme Court—what?—fifteen, twenty times. It seemed like half the First Amendment cases in Jasmine's con-law book had Pearson Payne listed as attorney of record.

"Tell me a little about Regent," Payne said, looking up at her. Jasmine thought she could detect the slightest hint of skepticism in his voice. She knew that in this firm, filled with Jewish lawyers and outspoken agnostics like Payne, all representing a bevy of liberal New York media clients, she should downplay the Christian and conservative aspects of her Virginia Beach law school.

"It's the Yale of the South," she replied, bringing a smirk to Payne's face. She had checked out his alma mater before she flew north for this interview. "In fact, we finished ahead of Yale in this year's moot court tournament." It was a not-so-veiled reference to the second-place finish in the national competition that Jasmine had featured prominently on her résumé.

"I see that," Payne said. "Congratulations." Jasmine nodded. "Looks like you've got a knack for second place," he quipped.

"Bad judging in the finals," Jasmine countered. She recrossed her legs. "Kind of like *New York v. Clarke*."

Payne didn't blink at the reference to his latest Supreme Court case—one he had lost by a five-four vote. "Touché," he said. "Sometimes those judges don't recognize brilliance when it's standing in front of them."

"My point exactly."

They talked a few more minutes about Regent, where Jasmine ranked second in her class, and about Payne's multi-faceted legal practice. Eventually Payne invited her to join him at the floor-to-ceiling windows that lined the outer walls of the office. They offered a spectacular view of Rockefeller Center. Jasmine could see, across the plaza, the studios for NBC's *Today* show, the Rockefeller Center ice-skating rink, the angels that lined the walkway to the plaza, and the eighty-foot-tall Norway spruce that had been chosen as this year's

Christmas tree. She was trying hard not to be impressed, but for a girl from Possum, Virginia, it was not easy.

"Thirty thousand bulbs on that baby," Pearson Payne said, pointing *down* to the Christmas tree. Though the tree was enormous, its top was still a good twenty stories below Payne's office. "The star on top is ten feet high."

"It's beautiful," Jasmine said. The view was breathtaking. She wondered if Payne ever got used to it.

"Mmm," Pearson replied. Then he turned to Jasmine as if reading her mind. "It's a great view, but we don't get much time to enjoy it. Eighty-hour weeks, incredible pressure, demanding clients." He paused and Jasmine nodded. She knew all this. "Why do you want to work here?" he asked, crossing his arms.

The bluntness of the question threw Jasmine off stride for a moment. But the man seemed to like the no-nonsense approach, so Jasmine decided to throw it back at him.

"I love constitutional law," she said. "Especially the First Amendment. And someday I want to sit on the Supreme Court." She watched Pearson's face carefully but detected no hint of disapproval or surprise. "For that, I need to work at a firm that argues the cases everyone else is talking about."

Pearson nodded. "And?"

Jasmine searched his eyes. *What was he hinting at? And . . . what?*

Clueless, she said the first thing that came to her mind. "And the money's not bad." For proper etiquette, she left the precise amount—$115,000 as a first-year associate—unsaid.

Payne smiled. "Exactly. I never hire anyone who is too dishonest to admit that money's a factor." He checked his watch.

It was nearly lunchtime, so Jasmine prepared herself for the next step in the interview dance—a power lunch. Her class standing and minority status had landed her several big firm interviews, though this was her first in New York City, and by now she knew the drill. Swanky restaurants and a ninety-minute lunch, as if lawyers took that much time every day. A high-profile partner like Payne would come along to make her feel important. It was a carefully choreographed performance, part interview and part recruiting. If the firm liked you, they would drop a job offer on you right after lunch. If not, they'd talk about how firm policy required that they run all candidates through their recruiting committee. They would promise to call you once you got back to school. A week or so later, you'd get a rejection letter in the mail.

Lunch was a big deal, and Jasmine was ready to graciously accept Payne's invitation.

"You bring any workout clothes with you?" Payne asked.

Huh? "Back at the hotel."

"Perfect!" Payne's eyes lit up. "Why don't I have Andre get a cab and escort you back there, then take you to the Downtown Athletic Club. I usually shoot a few hoops with some guys over lunch and then grab a pretzel or hot dog on the way back to the office. You in?"

"Sure," Jasmine said, faking enthusiasm. The thought of rubbing sweaty bodies with a bunch of out-of-shape old white guys was not exactly her idea of fun.

"It sure beats sitting around and drinking martinis," Payne said.

But Jasmine wasn't so sure.

18

4

NEARLY AN HOUR later, Jasmine was fed up. It had all started innocently enough. She and Pearson had been playing a friendly game of one-on-one in the stuffy little half-court gym at the athletic club. She even let the old guy score a few times. He wasn't half-bad, considering his age, though his feet barely left the floor on his "jumper." Jasmine resisted the urge to block every shot.

Then the pair from hell showed up.

The big guy, who introduced himself as David, was a real beast. About six-four and two-forty, the Beast had a bald head, hairy back, and sweat glands that started pouring out gallons of slimy perspiration two minutes into the game. By the end of game one, the Beast's shirt was soaked through, and sweat came flying off his head and back whenever he pivoted. Jasmine figured the Beast was somewhere in his forties, an old-school ballplayer who took himself entirely too seriously. His partner, a little guy called "Scooter," was probably fifteen years younger and fast as lightning. He handled the ball pretty well, and Jasmine guessed he had played some in high school, maybe even college.

The first game went smoothly, with Jasmine scorching the men from the outside as Payne smiled and ribbed the boys about getting beat by an old man and his "daughter." In game two, however, the Beast decided to get physical, taking Jasmine down on the blocks for a punishing game that resembled football more than basketball. The good-natured banter stopped, the pushing increased, and Jasmine and Payne got clobbered.

"Rubber match?" Pearson asked.

"Of course," the Beast snorted.

Game three was worse than the second game, in part because Jasmine was tired of backing down. It got particularly bad when Jasmine blocked one of the Beast's patented little hook shots.

"Whoa!" said Pearson, who didn't know when to shut up. "You blocked that baby into next week."

Jasmine gave her teammate a dirty look. He might be "the man" in a courtroom, but out here on the hardwood, he had to learn to let his playing do the talking.

Pearson's trash talking inspired the Beast to take the pushing and shoving to a whole new level, making life even more miserable for Jasmine. Two Beast elbows and one lowered shoulder later, Jasmine's competitive instincts took over.

She posted herself low on the blocks, established a broad

base, and held out her hand for the ball. As usual, the Beast leaned into Jasmine from behind, his elbow planted firmly in her back. Miraculously, Pearson managed to slide a bounce pass around the outstretched fingers of Scooter and into Jasmine's waiting hands. The last time she had the ball in this position, she simply took a quick step away from the Beast and swished a turnaround jump shot. She knew he expected that same move again. Instead, she gave him a head and shoulder fake that the Beast bit with every ounce of his 240-pound frame, hurling his body into the air to block her shot.

She had done this a thousand times, though she couldn't remember doing it on anyone quite so heavy before. Just as the Beast jumped, Jasmine dropped her shoulder and stepped hard toward the basket, going up and under the Beast, who rolled off Jasmine's back and landed with a thud on the floor.

The ball banked through. Jasmine thought she heard something snap as the Beast hit the deck behind her. She turned to see the Beast curled on the floor, holding his right elbow, while Pearson and Scooter walked to where he was lying. For a moment nobody spoke, and the only sound in the gym was the heavy breathing of the players and the echo of the ball as it bounced, then rolled to a stop.

Jasmine didn't move. She hadn't meant to hurt anyone. And now this out-of-shape, middle-aged white guy was lying on the floor with what might be a broken elbow, all because she couldn't keep her competitive instincts in check. Payne shot her a reproving look, and Jasmine figured she could kiss this job good-bye.

"You okay?" Payne asked the Beast, extending a hand.

The Beast reached out his left hand and rose to his feet,

shaking his head. "I guess so," he said, glancing at Jasmine. He straightened and bent his right arm a few times. "I don't think it's broken."

"Sorry about that," Jasmine said, though she didn't really feel sorry. She was glad that the brute's arm wasn't broken, but maybe this would teach him a lesson.

"Don't worry about it," the Beast replied, sweat dripping from his chin. He smiled and extended his right hand to shake Jasmine's. "I say we hire Jazz," the Beast said to Pearson.

"Me too," Scooter said, as Jasmine's jaw dropped in disbelief.

She looked from one conspirator to the next.

"I've always said you could learn more about a candidate in one game of basketball, golf, or tennis than you could in two days of interviews," Payne said. "That's why I always bring prospects to the gym or take them to the golf course." The old man broke into a full-fledged grin. "I want you to meet David Borden, one of my junior partners, and Scooter McCray, a senior associate." All three men were smiling.

"Based on today's performance," Pearson continued, "I think we'd rather have you with us than against us."

"I'll drink to that," the Beast said. And Jasmine knew that this time he wasn't putting her on.

Later that night, after Jasmine returned to her room at the downtown Hilton, she plugged her laptop into the hotel's broadband connection and accessed her e-mail. She was floating with the excitement of an offer from a major New York firm, news too wonderful to keep to herself. She sent a couple of e-mails to some law school friends, discreetly mentioning the offer from Gold, Franks. For the sake of modesty, she left out the precise amount of the salary, though she was pretty sure her friends already knew the ballpark for starting associates in New York mega-firms.

She also instant-messaged her little sister, a senior at Possum High, to tell her the good news. Ajori, too young to be worried about proper etiquette, instantly sent a return message marked by a teenager's enthusiasm: You rock! How much?

Jasmine smiled as she typed in her reply: $115,000 plus a signing bonus. She waited less than five seconds for Ajori's flashing response.

R U serious!!!! Can I get a loan????

No way, Jasmine typed back. You've got lousy credit.

While she continued the dialogue with her kid sister, Jasmine pulled up the Gold, Franks Web site and opened her in-box from school. Interspersed with the usual spam and forwarded messages from friends was an e-mail from the Regent professor who ran the school's legal aid clinic—Charles Arnold, legendary for his demanding teaching style and the street preaching he did on the Virginia Beach boardwalk. She opened it immediately.

Given the fact that you missed your rotation the last two weeks at the legal aid clinic, I have taken the liberty of assigning you a few indigent clients in need of representation. You can go by the clinic and pick up the case files this weekend. However, there is some urgency on one particular matter.

A former client of mine named Thomas Hammond has been subpoenaed for a federal court injunction hearing on Monday morning. He's not a named defendant but is a key witness in the case brought by the ACLU. I thought you might be interested since the issue is whether a crèche can be displayed in the town square of your hometown (Thomas is one of the live "Josephs" in the manger scene). He could use a lawyer to go with him and prepare him to testify. His home phone number is 757-432-0056. He doesn't have a cell phone.

You can appear under the usual third-year practice rules. If for some reason you need to address the court, the town attorney has agreed to serve as your "supervising" attorney for the day.

Have fun. And by the way, you might want to read *Lynch v. Donnelly* and *Allegheny County v. ACLU* before you go.

The legal aid clinic. It had seemed like such a good idea at the start of the semester. But her law firm interviews had caused her to miss a few rotations, and now, with the holidays and final exams approaching, she really didn't have time to fool with the likes of Thomas Hammond, a name that didn't ring any bells. She thought about her family's annual pilgrimage to the town square and the live manger scene. Why couldn't the ACLU just let the residents of Possum celebrate Christmas the way they always had?

Jasmine sighed, typed the case into her Outlook calendar, and clicked to open the blinking instant message from her sister.

Need a paralegal?

5

As the mayor of Possum testified, Jasmine Woodfaulk sat next to Thomas Hammond in the front row of the cavernous federal courtroom and studied the reaction of Judge Cynthia Baker-Kline. Because this was a request for a preliminary injunction that hinged primarily on legal issues, as opposed to factual determinations, there would be no jury in the box. Her Honor would be the sole decision maker. And Her Honor was not giving off good vibes.

Jasmine had heard her law school professors say you could sell tickets to any trial involving Judge Baker-Kline. Feared by most, the judge that lawyers called "Ichabod" combined a hair-trigger temper with a razor-sharp tongue that could slice up even seasoned litigators. She had a face that was all angles and bones—sunken eyes and a jutting jaw. Her reading glasses had crawled down her Wicked-Witch-of-the-West nose as the hearing progressed and were now hovering at the very end of that precipice, defying the laws of physics as they balanced there, mesmerizing Jasmine, who found herself wondering how they stayed.

Jasmine split her attention between the glasses and the telltale vein on the right side of Ichabod's neck that pulsed visibly when she got upset, like a barometer of her anger and angst, a warning to smart lawyers that it was time to change the subject. As Ichabod listened to the mayor's testimony, the vein pulsed in and out, in and out. Quickly. Grotesquely.

And Ichabod was scowling.

The mayor survived nearly an hour of pointed questions by Vince Harrod, attorney for the ACLU, and then a feeble attempt by the town's attorney to rehabilitate his testimony. Just when it looked like he might escape, the judge herself started in. "Who owns the Possum town square?" she asked the witness.

"The town does," the mayor responded in his high-pitched voice. "But Freewill Baptist Church maintains the manger scene."

"Do you charge Freewill Baptist Church any rent for the portion of the square where the manger scene sits?"

"No, ma'am." The mayor gave the town's lawyer a do-something look, but the lawyer appeared not to notice.

The mayor was a small man with a round face and a big handlebar mustache. Jasmine remembered the night he had handed out keys to the town at a banquet honoring Jasmine's state runner-up basketball team. Her teammates had dubbed him the "Munchkin Mayor," based on his resemblance to the character in *The Wizard of Oz.*

"And where might you attend church, Mr. Frumpkin?"

26

Ichabod leaned into the question, and the mayor's eyes went wide.

"Can she do that?" Thomas whispered to Jasmine. Jasmine just nodded.

A few seconds of silence followed as if the Munchkin Mayor had just been exposed in some mortal sin.

"Do you understand the question?" Ichabod scowled.

"Yes, Your Honor."

"Well?"

"I attend Freewill Baptist Church of Possum."

Ichabod made a check mark on her legal pad. She turned to Harrod. "The town council resolution authorizing a manger scene in the Possum town square for the holiday season—what exhibit number was that?"

"Exhibit 9, Your Honor."

"Please look at Exhibit 9," Ichabod instructed Mayor Frumpkin, "and tell me what that resolution says about who will maintain this manger scene on behalf of the city."

Bert Frumpkin pulled the exhibit out of the stack of papers in front of him, handling it carefully like the snake it had become. He took his time reading it, licking his lips a couple of times in the process.

"It doesn't say anything?" he finally responded.

To Jasmine, the mayor's answer sounded like a question, the way kids guess at an answer in class when they don't know, hoping the teacher might accept their humble offering.

"Then whose idea was it to delegate this responsibility to the good folks at Freewill Baptist Church?"

Frumpkin hesitated. "I'm not 100 percent sure."

This brought a glare from Ichabod that lowered the temperature in the courtroom five degrees.

"But it might've been mine," Frumpkin added.

"What a coincidence," Ichabod mumbled, which brought a smattering of chuckles from the reporters present.

She looked over the top of her glasses at the poor Possum mayor. "Did you ever consider asking Muslims to hold an Iftar on the Possum town square to celebrate the ending of their Ramadan fast or a Jewish rabbi to erect a menorah during Hanukkah?"

Frumpkin squirmed a little in his seat, and Jasmine could see the confusion in his eyes. Even she didn't know what an Iftar was—so there was no chance the mayor would.

"No," Frumpkin said, "but they're not national holidays either."

"That's right," Thomas whispered.

"Harrumph," Ichabod said.

She stared at the back wall for a second, then turned again to the witness. "Speaking of national holidays, Mr. Frumpkin, what did you do in your town square to celebrate Martin Luther King Day?"

"What's that got to do with anything?" Thomas wondered, loud enough so Jasmine could hear.

"Nothin' in particular this year," Frumpkin said.

"And in past years?"

"Actually, not much then either."

Jasmine winced at the implications. This case would not be good publicity for her hometown. The press would characterize Possum as Redneck City, USA.

"That's all the questions I have for this witness," Ichabod said, making one final check mark on her pad.

"For its next witness, the plaintiff calls Mr. Thomas Hammond," Harrod said.

6

JASMINE WATCHED HELPLESSLY as Vince Harrod fired
questions at Thomas Hammond for thirty minutes. In all the
trials she had watched as a law firm clerk, she had never seen
a witness look so ill at ease. The big man reminded her of
Shrek—squeezing into the witness chair with the wide-eyed
wonderment of an innocent ogre about to be swindled by a
crafty foe. Even his worn white shirt and blue blazer seemed
two sizes too small. He left the top button of his shirt unbut-
toned, relying on his tie to pull the collar somewhat together.
Jazz decided that Walmart shirts were not designed for necks
as thick as Thomas's.

Jasmine couldn't object to the questions because Thomas
was not a party, just a witness, and therefore she wasn't an

attorney of record in the case. The objections, such as they were, were being interposed by the Possum town attorney, Arnold Ottmeyer, a stooped and aging man who didn't appear to have much enthusiasm for protecting the witness. When he did object, rising slowly to his feet and raising his arm partway toward the judge like an orchestra conductor with an imaginary baton, it was too late to help the beleaguered witness.

"Mr. Hammond has already answered the question," Ichabod would say. "Objection overruled."

Thomas testified that he saw his role in the live Nativity scene as a ministry. He and Theresa would take every opportunity to pray with those who came to visit or talk to them about "the true meaning of Christmas."

"Did the town attorney or anyone else associated with the town ever tell you what you could or could not say to visitors?" Harrod asked.

"No."

"Did it ever occur to you that you were acting as a representative of the Town of Possum, and it would be inappropriate for you to proselytize people who came to visit the live manger scene?"

Ottmeyer stood and pointed his imaginary wand forward. "Objection. Assumes that the witness is a representative of the town."

Ichabod shot Ottmeyer an impatient glance. "Overruled."

A few questions later Harrod reviewed his legal pad and seemed satisfied that he had done enough damage with the witness. "No further questions," he announced.

"Nothing from me," Ottmeyer said with a big sigh.

Jasmine watched the tight lines on Thomas's face loosen just a little as he stood and stepped down from the witness stand.

"Where're *you* going?" Ichabod asked.

Thomas froze. "I, um . . . thought I was done."

Ichabod leaned forward. "I have a few questions as well," she said.

Resolutely, as if he were a gladiator being led to the floor of the Roman Coliseum, Thomas returned to his seat. He inhaled, then looked at the judge.

"So . . . I take it that you attend Freewill Baptist Church along with the mayor?" The way Ichabod phrased the question, it sounded like she was accusing Thomas of belonging to a cult.

He stiffened. "Yes, ma'am."

"Is it a big church?"

"Pretty big. 'Bout 150 members or so."

"I'll bet that you and the mayor probably know each other pretty well—probably bump into each other at church quite often?"

"We're in the same Sunday school class—" Thomas looked down at his hands for a moment—"but we don't really run in the same circles."

Ichabod studied her notes before peering at the witness again. "In that Sunday school class, do you ever discuss the live manger scene in the Possum town square and your efforts to proselytize people out there?"

Thomas furrowed his brow in confusion.

Ichabod shook her head at the density of the witness. "Do you ever talk in Sunday school about the manger scene?"

"Sometimes."

"Tell me about the last time you did so."

"Well, just last week, I might've mentioned a couple things." Thomas frowned and looked Ichabod squarely in the eye. "We prayed for a family I talked to at the manger last week . . . prayed that they might come to church and find out more about Christ." He swallowed. "And we prayed for you . . . that you would make the right ruling."

"You did?" A smirk pulled at the corner of Ichabod's mouth. "And what might that ruling be?"

Thomas shrugged. "Let us keep the manger scene up. Let us keep ministering to people."

"Did it ever occur to you," Ichabod snapped, "that trying to convert people to your Baptist faith on town property using a Christian manger scene sponsored by the town might violate the wall of separation between church and state?"

Jasmine had heard enough. This was so unfair! How could Thomas, with no legal training, answer such a question? She glanced at Ottmeyer to make sure he wasn't objecting—nope, he didn't even twitch—then she jumped to her feet.

"Objection!" she blurted out.

Ichabod turned her stare from Thomas to Jasmine. The judge took off her reading glasses and studied Jasmine as if figuring out the best way to torture the nervous young law student. "And who might you be?"

"Jasmine Woodfaulk. I represent Mr. Hammond."

"I see." Ichabod tented her fingers in front of her. "How long have you been practicing law?"

"I'm a third-year law student, and Mr. Ottmeyer is my supervising attorney today." Out of the corner of her eye, Jasmine noticed Ottmeyer turn partway around in his seat, shaking his head from side to side in quick, vigorous little motions.

"I see." The judge paused and Jasmine shifted from one foot to the other. "Then you probably haven't learned yet that you have to be a lawyer of record in the case to make an objection . . ."

"I know that, Your Honor, but—"

"Ms. Woodfaulk!"

"Yes, Your Honor."

"I wasn't finished."

"Sorry."

"In addition, even if you were counsel of record, it's typically not real smart to object to the questions of a judge who will ultimately decide the case. Is that clear?"

"Yes, Your Honor."

"Good. Now would you like to withdraw your objection?"

"I can't do that in good conscience, Your Honor."

"You 'can't do that in good conscience,'" Ichabod repeated. "And would you mind telling me why?"

Jasmine took a deep breath and tried to focus on the issue. Just like stepping up to the foul line . . . shut out the jeering fans, the trash-talking opponents . . .

"First, Mr. Hammond is not a lawyer and shouldn't have to answer legal questions about what is or isn't proper under the establishment clause. Second, if he were a lawyer, he'd probably point out that the phrase 'separation of church and state' is not found in the Constitution and is a poor metaphor for what the Founders actually intended to prevent—an officially sanctioned state religious denomination." Ichabod scowled at Jasmine, but it was too late for Jasmine to turn back now. "Third, and most important, Your Honor's question appears to ignore the fact that the U.S. Supreme Court previously ruled, in *Lynch v. Donnelly*, that the display of a crèche on a public square is constitutionally permissible."

When Jasmine stopped, she didn't like the fire she saw in Ichabod's eyes. "That's quite an objection, Counsel." The judge sneered. "Some might even call that a closing argument. But it's overruled for a few fundamental reasons."

Ichabod waved a document in her right hand. "This is the case of *Lynch v. Donnelly*. In that case a crèche was displayed on the town square with a number of other items, including a Santa Claus house, reindeer pulling Santa's sleigh, candy-striped poles, a Christmas tree, carolers, cutout figures representing a clown, an elephant, and a teddy bear, as well as a large banner that read, 'Season's Greetings.' Notice any differences so far?"

Before Jasmine could answer, Ichabod turned toward Thomas and continued her monologue. "Plus, the city in that case had a secular purpose for the decorations—depicting the historical origins of a national holiday. Now, Mr. Hammond, is the purpose of this live manger scene—of which you are a part—a secular purpose or does this live manger scene have a very religious purpose . . . insofar as you are concerned?"

"Objection!"

"Overruled."

"There's nothin' secular about the manger scene," Thomas stated. "The whole Christmas season ought to be spiritual, but this part certainly is."

Ichabod turned with glee back to Jasmine. "That, Ms. Woodfaulk, is one more reason your objection is overruled. I don't know what they teach in ethics classes these days, but back when I went to law school, they taught that you should never make a legal argument inconsistent with the testimony of your client."

"Mr. Hammond is not an official of the town," Jasmine shot back. The nerves had been replaced by competitive fire. "He doesn't speak for the town."

"And neither do you," Ichabod said. "So why don't you sit down and let the attorney for the town make his own objections. He's been practicing law long enough to know when they are proper."

Instead of sitting, Jasmine stood in defiance, staring at Ichabod for a few seconds—long enough to show she could not be intimidated, short enough so she could not be held in contempt. After she made her point, she took her seat.

"Thank you," Ichabod said. "Mr. Hammond, you may step down."

★

Following four full hours of testimony and the uninspired closing arguments of Harrod and Ottmeyer, Ichabod announced that she was ready to rule from the bench.

"The court is mindful that its ruling today will probably be misinterpreted and vilified by those on the religious Right—" Jasmine could swear that Ichabod looked right at Thomas and her—"but a judge has to do what's right, not what's popular. And this case is not even a close call.

"The court finds that the live manger scene displayed by the Town of Possum violates the separation of church and state required by our Constitution. Though the Supreme Court has previously upheld the right of a city to display a manger scene in its town square—that case did not involve sponsorship of a live manger scene with characters who go to the same church as the town mayor and see it as their Christian duty to proselytize visitors. The manger scene in *Lynch v. Donnelly* was one small part of a larger secular display. Though the Town of Possum has a few token secular symbols on its town square, the manger scene at issue here, like the one held unconstitutional by the Supreme Court in *Allegheny County v. ACLU*, is essentially a stand-alone display. As such, it smacks of a religious purpose and sends the message to any objective observer that the town government endorses orthodox Christianity."

Ichabod surveyed the courtroom audience and released an enormous sigh. "For the record, I personally enjoy the holiday season and celebrate the season in my own house with all the traditional Christmas displays—including a manger scene comprised of glass figurines that sits on my fireplace mantel. So this is no 'bah-humbug' ruling. But when the town uses public property to do the same thing, it violates the First Amendment of our Constitution and cannot be permitted. Accordingly, the injunction is granted."

Ichabod banged her gavel, gathered her papers, and stood.

"All rise," the clerk cried out.

"Unreal," Thomas mumbled. Jasmine instinctively put a hand on his arm and then, to her horror, watched as Judge Baker-Kline stopped in her tracks and spun to face him.

"Did you say something, Mr. Hammond?"

The tension nearly crackled as Thomas hesitated.

"No," Jasmine whispered. But she noticed Thomas take a deep breath and thrust out his jaw.

"I just can't believe that in the United States of America we can't even celebrate Christmas anymore."

The vein pulsed on Ichabod's neck as she considered her response. It seemed the entire courtroom—with everyone still standing—had sucked in a breath and didn't dare exhale. Jasmine thought her next step might be to contact a bail bondsman for her recalcitrant client.

"Mr. Hammond, one of the things that makes our country great is our religious freedom—the fact that our government can't tell you or me what god to worship. Now I realize that this ruling might disappoint you, and I believe that you're a sincere man in your firmly held beliefs. But, Mr. Hammond, you are sincerely wrong about this case . . ."

Jasmine could sense her client bristle next to her and half expected him to interrupt the judge.

"And what *I* can't believe," Ichabod continued, "is that in the United States of America, a town and a church would so blatantly disregard our cherished constitutional principles. Happy holidays, Mr. Hammond." Ichabod turned and left.

Jasmine's stomach rumbled. The look of determination on her client's face warned her that she probably hadn't seen the last of this showdown between the stubborn man who played Joseph and the grinch in the black robe.

7

As Jasmine drove, her headlights barely pierced the fog. She had left her law school apartment thirty minutes earlier, headed south on Centerville, crossed the Intercoastal Waterway, then headed southwest on Mount Pleasant Road and ultimately Indian River Road. The road snaked through swampland with cypress trees and thick underbrush on both sides, crossing the North Landing River twice, and finally emerging into the cornfields and soybean farms just outside Possum.

Jasmine took a deep breath as she approached the spot of *the accident*—the place where the entire school had erected an impromptu memorial for her dad three years ago. Students had placed flowers, pictures, and crosses on the side of the road. Virtually every player he ever coached placed an old pair of sneakers there. He had died instantly, according to the paramedics, crushed when he fell asleep and drifted over the center line, straight into the path of an 18-wheeler.

How many times had she driven past this spot? Sometimes it would conjure up emotions so real she could almost touch him. Other times she could force herself not to think about it. But tonight, in the loneliness of the fog, she didn't have a chance.

When she was little, she believed she would marry him. As a teenager she played ball for him, the smartest coach she ever had. In college, she would call him and listen to that baritone voice assure her that everything would be all right. Two torn ACLs, but still he said it would all work out. The funny thing is—she believed him.

And now he was gone, though his words stayed with her, motivating her still.

Stand up for what you believe in. If something's worth doing, it's worth doing right.

It was one of the reasons she found herself going to this meeting even though she had finals this week. Her dad would have been here if he were still alive.

She passed the curve in front of the paper mill and accelerated her little Neon, anxious to leave the pain behind. "I love you, Daddy," she whispered.

★

A few minutes later Jasmine pulled into the packed gravel parking lot of Freewill Baptist and smiled at the small marquee sign out front that announced tonight's meeting along with a thinly disguised message for Ichabod: *Your heart is an inn—do you have room for Jesus?* Freewill was an ultra-conservative congregation, a flock of true believers who had not yet embraced the contemporary worship styles and casual dress of their less-serious Christian brethren. Jasmine's family had always attended church on the other side of town, at the only African American church within ten miles, a small group of rowdy adherents who believed in marathon services and multiple offerings taken up by stern women wearing white gloves. But Jasmine's parents had shown her how to cross cultural barriers with ease—no small feat for a six-two African American woman who didn't exactly blend in with the crowd.

Jasmine found a parking spot, pulled on her long brown overcoat, and hustled toward the small box-shaped building with white siding where the faithful had gathered. She dodged the kids darting around the foyer and slipped into the small sanctuary with its stained-glass windows, dim lighting, and rows of wooden pews with cushions covered in red velvet. She didn't see any empty seats in the last few pews, so she found a spot against the back wall. Mayor Frumpkin was standing in front of the stage, pacing back and forth, talking excitedly. He waved around a copy of yesterday's *Virginian-Pilot*, with a headline that read "Possum Manger Scene Must Go—Town to Appeal."

"Arnold Ottmeyer says an appeal could take a year to get resolved," His Honor said.

This elicited a few groans from the audience. Jasmine heard someone toward the back mutter, "Lawyers" as if it were a curse word.

"If we rely on an appeal, we might as well kiss this Christmas good-bye and maybe the next one as well."

Though it didn't appear to Jasmine that the mayor was open to questions, a hand shot up anyway. He couldn't really ignore the man, so the mayor nodded in his direction. "Pete?"

A tall balding man in the second pew stood and turned so he could face the audience. Jasmine recognized the guy as a rabid fan from her high school basketball days. His face would turn beet red as he yelled at the refs, telling them they were missing a good game.

"Judicial tyranny," he said. "That's what this is."

Jasmine grinned to herself.

"You betcha," somebody said.

"Amen," said a little blue-haired lady sitting on the last pew, just in front of Jasmine.

"The only way to combat this is to get these tyrants removed from the bench . . . the same way our forefathers like Washington, Jefferson, and Patrick Henry got rid of the tyranny of King James." A few heads nodded.

A grandfatherly man standing next to Jasmine leaned toward her and whispered: "Pete Winkle. Fertilizer salesman. Teaches the adult Sunday school class here."

Jasmine nodded but thought to herself, *King James?*

"So I've got an impeachment petition that I took the liberty of drafting. I'd like to get a thousand signatures and send it to our congressman. I think that might get his attention." Jasmine noticed the little lady in the back pew go fishing in her pocketbook for a pen. "We've let these liberal judges rule our country long enough!" At this, Pete thrust his petition in the air, undoubtedly expecting a mob riot to break out.

Instead, there was a smattering of applause—a few clapped, but most just nodded.

"Well." The mayor fidgeted around up front as Pete settled in his seat again. "That's a good plan. Let's pass that petition around." Being a law student, Jasmine was half tempted to raise her hand and tell the mayor that the plan had the chance of Frosty in a Virginia summer, but she knew better. Based on her skin color, those who didn't know her would probably assume she was a liberal. No sense defending Ichabod and removing all doubt.

"But at the same time we're pursuing the impeachment option, I've got another plan that our town attorney tells me just might work." The mayor now had the rapt attention of the crowd and played to the spotlight. He twirled his mustache for a moment and then, to Jasmine's amazement, walked over to the front pew and pulled out a laptop. Within minutes a few helpers had erected a screen in front of the pulpit, and the mayor had hooked up his computer to an LCD projector. He punched a button on his remote and the first slide of his presentation—Operation Christmas Spirit—flashed brightly on the screen. *PowerPoint in Possum*, Jasmine thought. *What's the world coming to?*

The title slide dissolved and another took its place. "This," the mayor said, "is a diagram of the town square. . . ."

Partway through Mayor Frumpkin's explanation of his battle plan, Theresa Hammond, a plain woman with straight black hair, a prominent nose, and pale skin, moved her baby girl from one shoulder to the other. The infant opened her eyes for a moment, sucked hard on a pacifier, then laid her head back down on her mom's shoulder.

Her contentment lasted until the mayor hit a high point

in his presentation, drawing a smattering of applause that woke the little girl. This time she started fussing loud enough that Theresa had to slip out of the pew and head to the back of the church, shushing and patting her child the entire way. The movement seemed to calm the infant, and Theresa settled into a spot next to Jasmine, bouncing the child gently on her shoulder to keep the baby satisfied.

"She's a cutie," Jasmine said, hoping that Theresa wouldn't ask if Jasmine wanted to hold her.

"Thanks." Theresa glanced around and then edged a little closer to Jasmine. "I'm worried about Thomas," she said, her voice so low that Jasmine could hardly hear.

Jasmine raised an eyebrow.

"Did Professor Arnold tell you how he met us?" Theresa asked.

"Yes," Jasmine hesitated, missing the connection. She knew that her professor had defended Thomas and Theresa Hammond against negligent homicide charges in Virginia Beach when they failed to obtain timely medical help for their critically ill two-year-old son. Their belief in faith healing kept them from going to the hospital until it was too late. That was a year and a half ago. The Hammonds had since moved to Possum, changed churches, and added this newest family member. "But what's that got to do . . ."

"It's the same look," Theresa said. "When we were in court the other day . . . it was the same stubborn look that Thomas had when Joshie was sick—" Theresa stopped midsentence as Thomas slid out of his seat and started toward the women. She stopped patting her child for a moment and touched Jasmine's elbow. "Please don't let him do anything stupid."

"Okay," Jasmine said politely. "I'll do what I can."

Thomas joined the women and shook Jasmine's hand. "Is this gonna work?" he asked, nodding toward the mayor.

"I'm not sure," Jasmine whispered.

"I don't like it," Thomas said. His voice was low but tended to carry, eliciting a "shh" from the back row. "Too much hoorah. I like simple things at Christmastime, not so much sparkle and glitter."

Jasmine nodded and noticed Pete's hand shoot up.

"How do we know the NAACP won't file suit again?" Pete asked.

"It wasn't the NAACP that filed suit the first time," Jasmine blurted out before she could catch herself. Heads turned toward her and most of the crowd seemed to recognize her, prompting a few friendly smiles. The ones who didn't registered a fair amount of surprise, as if somebody had opened the belly of the Trojan horse and Jasmine had just crawled out. "The NAACP is the National Association for the Advancement of Colored People. They help protect the civil rights of African Americans," she explained. "It was the American Civil Liberties Union that filed suit, not the NAACP."

"Hard to keep all those liberal groups straight," somebody said.

"Folks, you remember Jazz Woodfaulk," the mayor said, seizing the moment. "She's gone from starring on the basketball court to starring in a court of law. She's just finishing up at Regent Law School, and we've been blessed to have her help defend the Town of Possum in this case."

Before Jasmine could correct the mayor and explain that she actually represented Thomas Hammond rather than the town, a few people said, "Amen," and several others started clapping. It wasn't much of an ovation, but it was better than Pete Winkle had managed with his Impeach the Judge petition.

"Do you think Operation Christmas Spirit will work?" somebody asked.

Jasmine hesitated. She saw hope in dozens of eyes. The mayor smiled expectantly.

"It's the best plan I've heard so far," Jasmine said.

"Praise the Lord!" said the little blue-haired lady in the back row.

8

Friday evening, December 8

The first sign of trouble was the half-empty parking lot. Jasmine remembered her senior year, the team that finished second in the state, and how the parking lot filled up early, half an hour before the girls' varsity game. If you got there late, like Jasmine had tonight, you might have to walk half a mile to the gym.

The population of Possum had hovered around four thousand people for the past several decades. During Jasmine's senior year, most every game had been standing room only— nine hundred screaming lunatics—and three times they had set up an overflow site in the school's auditorium. One of those nights, a village burglar, on the correct assumption that the entire Possum police force would be at the game, had vandalized more than a dozen homes and never been caught. It was a small price to pay, the locals said. The Lady Bulldogs had won.

Jasmine wrapped her overcoat around her lanky frame and entered the double doors to the gym. The familiar-looking lady at the table took Jasmine's five-dollar bill without looking up.

"How much are the programs?" Jasmine asked.

"One dol—" The lady's eyes went buggy. "Oh, my goodness! Jazz Woodfaulk!"

Jasmine blushed. This is what she hated about coming home.

The lady fished into her cash register and thrust the five-dollar bill back at Jasmine. "You don't pay to get into this gym, young lady." She stood, smiling the entire time, then leaned forward and gave Jasmine a hug. "You and your dad used to own this place."

"Thanks," Jasmine said, sheepishly trying to slip away.

"Enjoy the game, dear," the gatekeeper called out. "They could use you this year."

Jasmine stepped into the gymnasium and immediately sensed the apathy generated by a losing team. Pockets of fans were sitting in different spots on the bleachers, talking to each other, almost ignoring the game. Even the cheerleaders looked disinterested.

Jasmine eased past the well-wishers and villagers interested in discussing the manger case. She spotted her mother sitting with a few other team moms a few rows behind the home team bench, the same place she used to sit for Jasmine's games. Her mom was one of the few people in the gym leaning forward, hands on her knees, sputtering at the refs or the coach, intently following the game. Ajori was sitting on the bench, looking glum, talking to a teammate. Jasmine climbed into the bleachers next to her mom. "How's Ajori doing?" Jasmine asked.

"Two fouls. Both of 'em ticky-tack fouls."

"With just two fouls she oughta be in the game," Jasmine said.

The ref blew his whistle and Jasmine's mom threw her arms in the air. "That's ridiculous, Mr. Ref!" she yelled, rising to her feet. "You guys are pitiful!"

Coach Barker, a squat man with a buzz cut, shook his head and sauntered to where Ajori was sitting on the bench.

"No more reach fouls, Woodfaulk."

Ajori nodded.

"Get Kelley."

Ajori sprinted to the scorer's table and knelt in front of it. Just before she went in the game, Jasmine's mom called her name. When Ajori turned and saw Jasmine, her eyes lit up. The ref called her into the game and she hustled onto the court.

It took Ajori one minute, thirty-five seconds of playing time to get her shot blocked, followed by a three-second violation, and then to get called for going over the back on a defensive rebound.

"Kelley!" Barker shouted. "Get Woodfaulk."

Jasmine's stomach dropped as Ajori came slinking off the court and took a seat at the end of the bench. She stared at her shoes when Barker went to stand in front of her, yelling as he watched the game. "That's just a dumb foul, Woodfaulk! Stupid. You're a senior. I say, 'No fouls, Woodfaulk. Don't go over the back, Woodfaulk.' And what do you do? Bam!" Barker slapped his hands together. It seemed to Jasmine like the whole gym was listening. "You go over the back and pick up your third foul! That's just . . . that's just . . . moronic. That's what it is . . . moronic."

"He's a jerk," Jasmine whispered to her mom. Her mom's round face was flushed with anger, but Jasmine knew that her mom, one of the most outspoken women in all of Possum, would be loath to criticize the coach. When your husband is a coach and you experience all the critical comments and backstabbing from the parents, you make a vow not to do the same when your kid's playing.

But Jasmine had no such restraints. This was Barker's first year, and this was the first game Jasmine had seen him coach, but she had already heard about his antics. He had now turned his rantings from Ajori to some other poor kid on the floor who was apparently falling short in the hustle department.

"How can you stand this?" Jasmine asked.

"He's a little intense," Jasmine's mom admitted. "But what're you gonna do?"

★

"I can't believe he didn't play you the whole second half," Jasmine said to Ajori on the ride home after the game. Ajori was slumped in the passenger seat of Jasmine's Neon. She had hardly spoken.

"Can we not talk about it?"

"That guy is such an idiot. I mean, how can he sit out his best player the whole second half?"

Ajori turned on the radio while she riffled through Jasmine's CDs. "You need some new tunes, Sis. This stuff is ancient."

Jasmine switched the radio off. "What'd he say at halftime?"

Silence.

"C'mon, Ajori. What'd he say?" Jasmine had been amazed when the team had stayed in the locker room for only a few minutes at halftime. Then she stewed during the second half as her sister sat on the bench. Barker didn't make one substitution and hardly said a word, watching with his legs crossed and one arm resting on the back of the chair next to him as his team lost by thirty.

"If I tell you, can we not talk about the game anymore?"

"Okay."

Ajori took a deep breath. "He came in and ripped two sheets of paper from the stat sheets. Then he ripped that paper up into tiny slips and wrote everybody's name on a slip. As he folded them up, he said that we had played like crap—not his exact words—and it didn't really matter what he said or what he did since we didn't listen anyway. Then he said, 'As long as we're going to all play like a bunch of little old ladies, we ought to at least be democratic about it.' He put the folded papers in his hand and held his hand toward me. He told me to draw five and announce the names, which I did. Then he said, 'Ladies, those are your starters for the second half. The rest of you might as well make yourself comfortable on the bench.'"

"That's it?"

"Yep."

"I hate that man."

In response, Ajori turned on the radio again. "Me too," she mumbled.

"Dad never did anything like that."

Ajori responded with silence.

A few minutes later a change in subject matter loosened up Ajori, and by the time they hit the driveway, she was talking nonstop about the boys in her class. As Jasmine and Ajori climbed from the car, Ajori returned to the topic of basketball.

"Barker is making us practice at eight tomorrow morning," she said, hefting her gym bag over her shoulder. "He saw you at the gym and wants to know if you'll come and scrimmage with us."

Jasmine walked next to Ajori as they headed into the house. She wanted to be careful here—this was Ajori's team. She realized how hard it must be to be Jazz Woodfaulk's little sister in a town like Possum, especially when you're four inches shorter and born without the Woodfaulk basketball gene.

"How do you feel about that?" Jasmine asked.

"I don't care," Ajori shot back. "I won't be there. I'm quitting."

9

A few minutes before eight on Saturday morning, Jasmine found herself lacing on an old pair of sneakers in the cramped driver's seat of her red Dodge Neon. She could barely squeeze herself into the seat to drive, much less bend around the steering wheel and put on her treads. Ajori was having less difficulty in the passenger seat, though she hadn't muttered a word yet. Under ideal circumstances on a Saturday morning, Ajori would have slept in until noon and stayed in her pajamas until two.

Jasmine and her mom had talked Ajori out of quitting the night before. It was the third time this season Ajori had announced she was going to quit, according to Jasmine's mom. Jasmine at first decided not to come to practice but changed her mind late last night as she tossed and turned in bed, feeling sorry for her little sister. She would show Barker a thing or two during practice. Afterward she would take the opportunity to pull him aside and casually give him a few pointers about the game.

Nobody should treat her little sister the way Barker did.

It was 8:15 before Barker showed up in his Ford pickup, a gun rack and American flag covering the back windshield. He opened the gym, rolled out the balls for the girls to warm up, then disappeared into his office.

"Where's he going?" Jasmine asked Ajori.

"Smoke break."

The scrimmage didn't start until nine. Barker placed Jasmine with the second team and put eight minutes on the clock. "Call your own fouls," he said.

For the first few minutes, the starters actually showed sparks of potential. Ajori hit a couple smooth jump shots, and a tall, lanky white girl named Ginger pulled down a few rebounds when she wasn't busy pulling her long blonde hair back into a tight ponytail. Ginger was probably six feet tall and might have been a good post player, except that she didn't have a competitive bone in her body. She was quite possibly the nicest player Jasmine had ever played against. "Sorry," Ginger would say if she touched Jasmine on a shot. "My bad" when a teammate's pass would sail through her hands. And when Jasmine boxed her out, Ginger would simply move out of the way, as if physical contact with another player might result in some deadly communicable disease.

"Congratulations," Barker said to Ginger at one point in

the scrimmage. "You get the least production out of six feet in height of any player in women's basketball."

"Sorry," Ginger said.

The only African American on the team other than Ajori, a little water bug named Tamarika, took care of the ball-handling responsibilities. In one particularly nice sequence, Ginger grabbed a rebound and threw an outlet pass to Tamarika. The quick little guard scooted around a few of Jasmine's helpless teammates and drove right at Jasmine. At the last possible second, just as Jasmine went up to block Tamarika's shot, the kid dished a no-look pass to Ajori, who banked in a nice jump shot. Barker immediately blew his whistle, stopping the scrimmage so he could yell at a few of Jasmine's teammates. He never complimented the starters on their nice play.

Jasmine took advantage of the coach's rantings to bend over, hands on her knees, and suck in a few deep breaths. *Law school and basketball don't mix,* she thought. But she also wondered how this team could look so pitiful in the game and have such brilliant moments in practice.

"You ladies better give Woodfaulk some help defensively," Barker screamed at Jasmine's teammates. "You can't expect her to do it all! She's got two bad knees and she's out of shape." Jasmine jerked her head up and gave Barker the eye, which he ignored. "Plus, she's carrying around a few more pounds than she did in college."

Jasmine dominated the next several minutes. She drove the lane, crashed the boards, and blocked one of Ajori's shots back to half-court. Barker's shrill whistle brought her out of the zone. This time he turned his ire on the starters.

"This is what happens every game," he complained. "The

other team starts running on us and we lose control . . ." He stared at Ajori and Tamarika. "We start playing hip-hop basketball, totally undisciplined."

What's that supposed to mean—"hip-hop" basketball? Jasmine was liking Barker less by the second.

"This isn't the WNBA," Barker continued. "I want three passes before you shoot or I'll tie up the nets for the rest of practice like I did last week!"

Ajori rolled her eyes. Tamarika stared at a spot on the floor, shifting from one leg to the other. "My bad," Ginger said.

The next time down the floor a fired-up Ajori blocked Jasmine's shot and passed to Tamarika. Several passes later, after working the ball around like a Princeton basketball team from the 1950s, Ajori scored over the outstretched arms of Jasmine.

When Jasmine posted up in the lane at the other end of the floor, Ajori gave her sister a sharp elbow in the ribs. "Quit trying to make me look good," Ajori sneered. "I don't need your charity."

Sheesh, Jasmine thought, *are we having fun yet?*

★

An hour later, as the girls were running their suicide drills, Jasmine walked over and stood next to Coach Barker. "Thanks for scrimmaging, Woodfaulk," he said. "It helped our kids see their weak spots."

"Sure."

He blew the whistle and Jasmine felt like it had pierced her eardrum. "Two more!" he shouted. The girls groaned.

Jasmine thought about the American flag proudly displayed in the back window of Barker's truck. In her trial-practice class, she had learned to communicate in a language the jury understood. She'd try it out on Barker.

"Know what makes this country great?" Jasmine asked as she and Barker watched the girls jog up and down the court on their next suicide. Ajori was near the back of the pack.

"What?"

"Hard work and freedom," Jasmine said. "If you don't have freedom, you're like Communist Russia used to be. If you don't have hard work, you're France."

Barker coughed, the phlegmy variety common to smokers, never taking his eyes off the court. "Your point is?"

"Basketball teams are the same way. Right now, this feels like Communist Russia, Coach." Another piercing whistle and the girls started on their last suicide. "You've got to give them some freedom to play."

"Is that so?"

The two stood there in silence until the girls limped across the baseline at the conclusion of their last suicide. "Gather round," Barker said.

The girls hobbled over huffing and puffing. Most of them bent over, hands on knees.

"What are the rules for when your parents whine about your playing time?" Barker asked.

"You don't play the next game," Ginger said between hard breaths.

"That's right," Barker said. "And, Tamarika, what happens when your parents complain to me about my coaching?"

Tamarika mumbled something that Jasmine couldn't hear.

"That's right," Barker said. "Double suicides." He turned to Ajori. "You think that rule applies to big sisters?"

Ajori groaned.

"On the baseline, ladies," Barker announced. "You're about to find out."

"This is stupid," Jasmine said as she walked toward the baseline with them. If she had been the cause of their running, she could at least share in their pain.

The girls lined up on the baseline and Barker walked in front of them. "Any more suggestions before we start running?" he asked Jasmine.

The other girls looked at Jasmine like they might tar and feather her if she said a word.

"No, sir," Jasmine shot back. "Stalin would be proud."

10

SATURDAY EVENING, DECEMBER 9

Thomas Hammond had never seen so much junk in the Possum town square in his life. It felt to him more like the flea market than a celebration of Christmas. For starters, he didn't like the big sign at the front: "The History and Traditions of Xmas." As if you couldn't even say the name of Christ anymore.

What's America coming to?

As one of Theresa's cousins watched the kids, Thomas and Theresa manned their live manger scene in a back corner of the square, though tonight it seemed more like a petting zoo. There were crowds of children waiting in line—*waiting in line!*—to pet the animals. And hardly anyone paid attention to the doll baby cradled in Theresa's arms. Even if they did, Thomas and Theresa were under strict instructions not to say anything that might be construed as proselytizing. Same for the carolers, who were under orders not to sing any serious Christmas carols, just stick with the "We Wish You a Merry Christmas" stuff. No telling who might be spying for the ACLU.

To make matters worse, the manger scene stood right next to the Twelve Days of Christmas display. The twelve drummers drumming were putting the animals on edge, not to mention Thomas. But he would gladly suffer through another hundred drummers drumming if he could just get rid of the ten lords a-leaping—ten grown men wearing tights who periodically put on a little leaping and dancing display with the nine ladies dancing. After watching the first performance, Thomas was pretty sure that there ought to be a law against men with beer guts wearing tights. Meanwhile, the eight maids a-milking, which Thomas thought was one of the calmer parts of the display, drew a constant chorus of "yuck" and "gross" from the schoolchildren who dropped by. Hadn't those kids ever seen a cow udder before?

The mayor scurried over, and Thomas stepped away from the animals to talk with him.

"We've got a problem," Frumpkin confided.

Since when does the mayor discuss town problems with me? Thomas wondered.

"It's Santa Claus." The mayor motioned with his head toward the St. Nick line—easily the longest on the square. At the moment there was nobody in Santa's chair. "Bo Barton's sick. But he didn't bother telling anyone 'cause he wanted to do this so bad. He's been coughin' and wheezin' all over the kids. 'Bout had a revolt from the parents."

The mayor glanced around and inched a half step closer. "Then Bo flipped his beets."

Thomas made a face. "Was a kid sittin' on his lap?"

"Of course," the mayor said. "But at least Bo had the good sense to turn his head to the side. Said he didn't get a lick of stuff on the kid, but the parents weren't so sure. I know this much, that Santa Claus suit will need a good washin' later."

"That is a problem," Thomas offered.

"Bo's a big man," the mayor continued. "Didn't need no paddin' or anything. And I need somebody who can take his place right away."

Whoa, Thomas thought as it dawned on him where this was headed. He started shaking his head. "No way," he said. "Get one of those dancing lords to do it."

"They're too skinny, Thomas."

Thomas tilted his head a little and gave the mayor a skeptical look.

"Okay, they're not exactly skinny. But they've got these soft little guts and skinny legs. But you—you've got real bulk. You're the only guy around here right now who can fill out that suit."

"I'm Joseph," Thomas protested.

"I can be Joseph," the mayor said.

Thomas crossed his arms and shook his head. "Mayor, I want to help ya, but I don't even let my own kids believe in Santa. Christmas is about Jesus, not Santa."

The mayor sighed in frustration. Thomas felt sorry for the little man, but this was a matter of principle. You didn't ruin a good manger scene just to get a fat Santa.

At that moment, with both men at a loss for what to do next, destiny intervened. They noticed him at the same time—the perfect solution. He was a large man with a wonderfully round belly and, as if he had been preparing for this role his whole life, a long and straggly gray beard!

They spotted him as he wandered toward the Frosty the Snowman display. Thomas raised his eyebrow at the man, and the mayor smiled. "Do you know his name?" Frumpkin asked.

"Nah," Thomas said. Like most other residents of Possum, he had periodically seen the man roaming the streets in the same tattered clothes; then he would disappear for long periods of time, presumably to roam the streets in the big city of Norfolk. Thomas and his kids had bought the man a sub on a couple of different occasions. Everyone around town called him the Possum bum.

The mayor shrugged and walked toward the guy. "Hey, buddy, you got a second?"

★

Jasmine had studied all afternoon. By evening she needed a break. Besides, she wanted to see this spectacle for herself. She bumped into the principal of Possum High School next to the fruitcake stand. "Can I ask you a question?" Jasmine asked.

"Sure, Jazz."

Jasmine looked around. "It's kind of private. Can we step over here for a minute?"

Jasmine pulled the man away from the card tables loaded with an assortment of fruitcakes, destroying the theory that there was really only one fruitcake in the world that just got passed around from one person to the next.

"It's about Coach Barker," Jasmine began. She shuffled her feet a little, trying to think of an acceptable way to say this.

Jasmine had always liked her high school principal. Her fondest memory of Mr. Greenway was the time he caught Jasmine skipping class. He jettisoned his normally sunny disposition for about fifteen minutes as he raked her over the coals. She had never seen such fire in Greenway's droopy eyes before. When he was done with his lecture, he considered his options out loud. "I could suspend you for tonight's game," he said. Jasmine remembered how her stomach sank to her knees. "Or I could just call your father and let him know." Her stomach flipped. "Or I could tell you that you'd better go out and win tonight's game by thirty to make it up to me."

They won by thirty-five.

"I don't know how to say this diplomatically," Jasmine continued. "So I won't. Barker's destroying the girls' basketball program." She watched Greenway's face for a reaction but saw none. Every good principal knows how to keep a poker face. "He humiliates the girls every chance he gets and tries to get them to play this slow-down game. I mean, it's just not good Possum basketball."

"What do you suggest?" Greenway asked.

"Talk to him." Since she'd gone this far, Jasmine might as well say what she thought. "If he doesn't change, fire him in midseason. Ajori only gets one senior year, and he's ruining it."

Greenway pursed his lips. He waited long enough for Jasmine to get uncomfortable—another principal trick. "Who would I get to coach them?" he asked.

The question caught Jasmine a little off guard. She was ready to make a case for Barker's firing, not suggest a new coach. She mentally ran down a list of teachers she still knew at Possum High. Then she thought about the townspeople. "I don't know," she said at last. "What about Rebecca Arlington?"

Greenway frowned at the suggestion of the assistant coach taking over. "Rebecca didn't even play ball in high school. She's just there so the girls have somebody to talk to. And our JV coach doesn't want to move up." Greenway hesitated. "I already asked her."

The implication threw Jasmine further off stride. "You did?"

"Yeah. Barker already tried to quit once."

What a loser! The guy's not even halfway through his first season as head coach.

"Well, it seems to me that anybody would be better than Barker," Jasmine offered.

Greenway took a half step closer. "You ever think about coaching, Jazz? You'd be great."

"You're kidding, I hope."

"I'm dead serious. The girls would respect you. The town would rally around. Rebecca could stay on as your assistant."

Jasmine immediately thought of a million reasons it could never work. "I'm in my third year of law school, I've got—"

"Take a semester off," Greenway suggested.

"It's not that easy. I've got a big offer from a New York law firm, contingent on graduating in May. Besides, I'm not looking for a job. This is about Ajori and her teammates, not me."

"That's the problem," Greenway said. "We've just started the season and everybody already thinks Barker ought to go, but nobody has a better solution. Listen, Jazz, your dad put this program on the map. How great would it be if his daughter came back and rebuilt it?"

"Barker just needs someone to hold him accountable," Jasmine retorted. She wanted to help her little sister, but she had no desire to step back in time and return to Possum as a girls' basketball coach. She was going to be a lawyer now. A good one. Why couldn't people understand that?

"I hear you," Mr. Greenway said. "But at least you can understand some of the challenges I'm facing. It's hard to hold a guy accountable when he doesn't even want the job in the first place."

"That's why you get paid the big bucks," Jasmine said, thinking about how much more she would make in her first year than Mr. Greenway was making after thirty or forty years of experience. Certainly much more than she would ever make as a basketball coach.

But it wasn't about the money, she assured herself. It was about breaking out and becoming successful in the real world. It was about facing the challenges of New York City. And besides, she wasn't sure Ajori would listen to her even if Jasmine did coach. She had a great relationship with her little sister. Why jeopardize that?

"Think about it," Greenway said. "But keep this conversation confidential."

"I will."

"You can't share it with anyone—not even Ajori."

"I know."

11

Six-year-old John Paul Hammond, nicknamed "Tiger" by his parents for obvious reasons, had slipped away from the loose babysitting of his mom's cousin and raced around the Possum town square on a candy-cane sugar high. He eventually snuck his way into the Santa line, stealing nervous glances in the direction of his parents to make sure they weren't looking.

Though the line took forever, Tiger hung in there and waited his turn. When he finally got to the front of the line, he took one final glance at the manger scene and a quick look around for his babysitter. The coast was still clear. The little baby who had been in line ahead of Tiger was now sitting on Santa's lap, refusing to look at the mom trying to take a picture. Suddenly the baby began to howl as if Santa had tortured her, and Santa immediately handed the kid back to her mom.

Tiger scurried up and jumped on Santa's lap. "Are you real?" Tiger whispered. Santa sure smelled real, at least as real as the manger animals after a good rain.

"Ho, ho, ho," Santa mumbled as if he were tired of hearing his own voice.

Tiger decided to give the beard a little tug as a quick test.

"Ouch," Santa said, this time with a little more energy. "You better watch it, young man, or I'll put you on the naughty list."

Whew. That must mean I'm on the nice list for now. "Sorry," Tiger said.

"Just don't let it happen again," Santa warned. "Now what's your name, little man?"

"Tiger."

"I should have known," Santa said. "You been good, Tiger?"

This was a tricky question. Tiger didn't want to fib, but the truth could mean coal in his stocking. "Kinda."

"Well," Santa said, and Tiger found himself turning his head a little to the side, so Santa's bad breath didn't blow right into Tiger's nose, "you give any money or food to homeless people this year?"

Tiger scrunched his little brow, trying to remember. "I think so, Santa."

"Good, then you're on my good-boy list. Now whadya want for Christmas?"

That was easy. Tiger leaned forward so he could whisper

in Santa's ear. He knew that this would be the ultimate test of whether Santa was real. Tiger's mommy and daddy, who claimed to be the ones who bought all the presents, would never get him this.

"Mmm," Santa said. "I'll see what I can do."

"Really?" Tiger asked.

"Has Santa ever lied to you before?"

Tiger didn't have to think long on this one. He'd never even talked to Santa before. Thankfully, he'd never had to smell the old guy before, either.

"Nope."

"Good, then he's not going to start now."

His task complete, Tiger started to climb down from Santa's lap, but Santa held on to him for a moment. "You know what the real meaning of Christmas is?" he asked.

"Yes, sir," Tiger said, grateful for such an easy question. His daddy had drilled this into Tiger every night for the last week. "That Jesus came down to earth 'cause He loved us."

"And?"

Tiger hunched his shoulders. That was it, as far as he knew.

"And was born in a manger because there was no room for Him in the inn," Santa said, spewing his stinky breath everywhere.

Oh yeah, Tiger thought. *Now can I get down?*

"So it's really about homelessness," Santa continued. "Jesus was homeless, and He wants us to give gifts to the homeless."

Wow. Tiger wrapped his mind around the idea. *I never thought of that.*

The night was nearly over by the time Vince Harrod approached Thomas Hammond with another subpoena. Thomas took the document, stared at Harrod with thinly veiled contempt, then finally looked at the papers in his hand. This time the subpoena required Thomas to attend court on Monday, December 11, at 9 a.m. in Judge Cynthia Baker-Kline's courtroom.

"You know the drill," Harrod said.

"I sure do," Thomas replied as he turned to survey the manger area for sheep droppings.

12

Monday, December 11

Thomas sat stiffly in the front row of the courtroom. This was a travesty! First, Harrod had examined Mayor Frumpkin for nearly an hour. Now the judge was taking her turn pummeling the poor man. And all the while the town's attorney just sat there, scribbling notes on a legal pad, not even looking at the witness.

Thomas wished that Jasmine could be here—at least she would say something! But she had a final exam this morning that she couldn't get moved, leaving Ottmeyer to fend for himself.

"So you're saying that this was just a secular holiday

71

display about Christmas and not an attempt to get around my earlier ruling?" Ichabod leaned toward the witness.

Frumpkin shifted in his seat. "Judge, we weren't trying to get around your earlier ruling—we were trying to comply with it. I mean, the sign didn't even say, 'The History and Traditions of Christmas.' It said, 'The History and Traditions of Xmas.'"

Ichabod frowned. "The easiest way to comply with my ruling is to keep the crèche off the town square." She let out a sigh as if she detested where this case was taking her. "Who was the architect of Operation Xmas Spirit?" she asked. Under questioning from Harrod, Ottmeyer had referred to his scheme as Operation Xmas Spirit rather than Operation Christmas Spirit.

"I was."

"In putting together the plan for this celebration, did you happen to read the Supreme Court's opinion on the Ten Commandments cases handed down just this summer?"

Frumpkin's hesitation told Thomas that the mayor had indeed read it. But like many politicians, Frumpkin wasn't about to let the facts stand in his way. "No, Your Honor."

"Then you may be interested to know that in the case of *McCreary v. ACLU*, one of the things the Court considered was the history of the Ten Commandments display and whether it demonstrated an improper religious purpose by the county officials. In that case, the county first hung just a framed copy of the Ten Commandments on a courthouse wall all by itself and only later, after the display was challenged by the ACLU, did they add other historical documents like the Magna Carta. That's what you've done here—tried to camouflage a religious display by adding secular elements to it. And in this case—with a live manger scene and the potential for proselytizing still there—it also remains a fundamentally religious display, doesn't it?"

Frumpkin made a face as if the argument had never occurred to him. "With all due respect, Your Honor, I have to disagree. This was just a straight-up display of history and traditions."

"Was it?"

Frumpkin squirmed for a moment but then rallied. After all, he knew where the voters stood on this issue. "That's all it was, Judge. A fair and balanced view of the history and traditions of the holiday."

"I see." Ichabod leaned back in her chair and reviewed some notes. The silence hung like a guillotine over the courtroom.

"Well then, it would be important for the display to accurately reflect the holiday traditions and history. So let's start with this question: how far back did you go?"

"Huh?"

"How far back did you trace the history of Christmas? Who did your historical research?"

Frumpkin twitched his nose at the question. He took a quick drink. "We went back hundreds of years, Judge. To a time when Christmas wasn't commercialized like it is today. And I guess I was pretty much the one doing the research."

"I see."

This time Frumpkin waited through the silence, though he squirmed so much he reminded Thomas of fishing, the way a worm would wiggle around as you skewered it with the hook.

"So you were aware that the church first began celebrating

Christmas on December 25 in reaction to the Roman pagan festival honoring Saturn, the god of peace and plenty?" Ichabod eyed the silent witness with amusement. "And I'm sure you were aware that the Roman holiday called Saturnalia was one of the most pagan and debased celebrations ever imagined."

"I'm not really up to speed on Saturnalia," Frumpkin admitted. "When I said 'history,' I was actually referring to as far back as the colonial time frame."

"Oh," Ichabod replied. "Then I'm sure you had a display someplace on the square commemorating the fact that the Puritans banned any celebration of Christmas when they landed in the New World in the 1600s. As you know, anyone caught celebrating Christmas in the New England colonies would be subject to arrest and fines."

"Um . . . I didn't happen to run across that one law by the Puritans."

"Oh, it wasn't just one law." Ichabod had a look of smug satisfaction on her face that was driving Thomas nuts. "You see, Mayor Frumpkin, similar laws were passed through-out the colonies, and Christmas wasn't celebrated until the Revolutionary War. You know why?"

"My research didn't exactly reveal why."

"Because the celebration of Christmas by Christians in Europe had become almost as bad as the celebration of Saturnalia by the Romans. And the Puritans didn't want any part of it. Take for example, Christmas carolers. Did you have any of those in your town square celebration?"

"Yes, Your Honor."

"Well, that tradition is centuries old. In England during the days of King Charles, drunken mobs would roam the streets in a tradition that was a cross between Halloween and Mardi Gras. These mobs would bang on the doors of the houses of aristocrats and demand food, drink, and money. If they didn't get it, they would loot these nice homes and carry away everything inside."

Frumpkin's eyes were wide with amazement. This was obviously not the type of history he had in mind.

"My law clerk researched all this," Ichabod continued. "It's publicly available on the Internet."

Thomas had always hated the evil Internet for a number of reasons. Now he had one more.

"The song 'We Wish You a Merry Christmas' originated during this era. Mobs would go from rich house to rich house and sing 'so bring us some figgy pudding.' Then they would follow it with a threat: 'We won't go until we get some . . . so bring some out here!' Did you realize that, Mr. Frumpkin?"

By now nobody in the courtroom was surprised when Frumpkin simply shook his head.

"And did you know that as late as 1828, in New York City, they had to hire a whole additional police force to guard against Christmas looters on December 25?"

"No," Frumpkin answered. "But that doesn't surprise me. After all, New York City is New York City."

Got that right, Thomas thought.

"And also," Ichabod said, undeterred, "let me ask you a few questions about your use of the term *Xmas.*"

"Okay." Frumpkin scooted a little forward in his seat as if he was finally on solid ground.

"Do you know why that term is used?"

"Yeah. Retailers and such decided that they couldn't use

the name of Christ anymore because it wasn't politically correct."

Ichabod studied Frumpkin for a moment, sizing him up. "Yes, but do you know where the word *Xmas* originated?"

Frumpkin scrunched his face and thought. It seemed to Thomas that the little mayor was growing weary of admitting his ignorance. "Sure," he said. Though he didn't offer any details.

"Then you know," Ichabod said, "that it actually originated with the Greek followers of Christ during the time of Roman persecution. The Greek word for the name of Christ is X-R-I-S-T-O-S. Like the symbol of the fish, the letter *X* became a powerful symbol for the early Greek Christians, especially Christians being persecuted for their faith. The letter *X* would often be used to mark the spot where a martyr died. So when Christmas celebrations started in this country, the use of the term *Xmas* served as a powerful reminder of both the birth of Christ and the martyrs who paid the ultimate price in the first century to spread the faith."

"Interesting," Frumpkin said.

"So you see, Mr. Frumpkin, even the use of Xmas on the sign at the front of the square could lead a reasonable judge to conclude that you were just using an ancient symbol of the Christian faith as a way to trick me into thinking you had secularized the celebration."

A reasonable judge, Thomas thought. *Wonder where we could find one of those?*

Thomas had the urge to stand up and tell this judge a thing or two. Though he didn't know much about court proceedings, he was pretty sure that Harrod wouldn't be calling him as a witness today. Frumpkin had already given away the farm, and Harrod wouldn't need Thomas. He was equally sure that Ottmeyer wouldn't be calling him to testify, since Ottmeyer looked like he just wanted to get out of the courtroom as soon as possible.

So, Thomas reasoned, his only chance to be heard, his only chance to say how utterly ridiculous this all was, would be if he stood up right now and spoke his mind. What could they do to him—throw him in jail?

Then another thought hit him. Something more effective. More controversial. The judge had inspired him with her little speech about Christian martyrs. *It's about time somebody stood up to our own government,* Thomas thought.

It's about time to put the X back in Xmas.

Jasmine left her exam and headed straight for her apartment, calling Ottmeyer's cell phone on the way. She left a message with the town attorney and another on the Hammonds' home answering machine. While driving, she flipped from one radio station to another but couldn't find anything about the hearing. It was driving her crazy not to know.

She grabbed the remote as soon as she got inside her apartment and started flipping through the channels before even removing her winter coat. The noon news had just started and the nice-looking brunette on channel 3 led off with the manger story.

"In a controversial ruling issued just minutes ago, Judge Cynthia Baker-Kline deemed another holiday display on the Possum town square unconstitutional. Her ruling has infuriated conservative activists, who claim that Baker-Kline has ignored controlling Supreme Court precedent and distorted the very history of Christmas."

Wording from the Court's opinion suddenly filled the screen as the anchor read along. "'The Puritans outlawed Christmas celebrations because they thought the birth of Christ was too sacred an event to be associated with such a secular celebration,' Judge Baker-Kline wrote. 'Likewise, I am convinced that Christmas is, by definition, a religious holiday celebrating the nativity of Christ. I also find that the Possum town square celebration in question, though it had many secular trimmings, was still a religious display on public property. Like the Puritans, I find myself constrained to rule it illegal.'"

The news then flashed to video footage of Pete Winkle soliciting signatures for his Impeach the Judge petition. "It's judicial tyranny plain and simple," Winkle was saying. "And I don't care what the Puritans did."

Five minutes later Theresa Hammond called and confirmed that things were every bit as bleak as the television news made them out to be. "You've got to talk with Thomas," she said. "He said he's not going to take the court's ruling lying down."

13

Thomas arrived at the town square while it was still light. The night before, he and Theresa had been up until two in the morning tracing and cutting life-size manger figures out of plywood. Though Theresa hadn't been happy about it, she had done a wonderful job painting the donkey, the sheep, the ox, the shepherd, and of course, the Virgin Mary. In Thomas's opinion, the Virgin Mary looked a little bit like one of Cinderella's ugly stepsisters, but other than that, the figures were easily recognizable. Besides, Scripture never said that Mary was easy on the eyes.

He carted the plywood figures out of his truck and attached wooden bases made of two-by-fours in the shape of an X. As he hauled the figures over to his usual spot on the square, carrying two at a time, the shepherd slipped from Thomas's grasp and landed on the hard ground right on the crook of the shepherd's staff, snapping the plywood at a particularly thin point. Fortunately, Thomas had a few rolls of duct tape kicking around in the back of his truck, and it didn't take him any time at all to fix the staff.

Around 5:30, just as darkness was falling, Thomas placed Bebo in the makeshift straw-lined cradle that he had built out of old two-by-fours and leftover pieces of plywood. He turned on the spotlight that he had hooked up to a Walmart car battery and took his place next to the plywood Mary.

A few folks who had watched him assemble his set told him how nice it looked. For some reason, they hung around after Thomas turned on the spotlight, perhaps waiting to see if he might be thrown in jail. Soon they were joined by a few other passersby. As folks gathered, many would tell him what a great idea this was. Others would remark about how this would really show that federal judge a thing or two. The townsfolk snapped pictures as if the manger scene were a national monument.

"You got a permit for that?" one of the men asked.

"Do you even need a permit?" someone else inquired.

"I'd just hate to see that judge get him on a technicality," the first guy said.

"Did Mary and Joseph have a permit?" Thomas asked. Since nobody seemed to have an answer, that was the end of the discussion.

Cell phone lines in Possum started buzzing, and word spread quickly. Soon the crowd had grown to nearly a hundred folks. Someone started singing "Away in a Manger," and the entire group of onlookers joined in. After a few more phone calls, an entrepreneurial villager arrived with a card table, a pot of hot apple cider, and a hundred Styrofoam cups. He sold the cider for a buck a cup so he didn't have to make change.

Eventually the mayor himself joined the throng and started singing, shaking hands, and patting the heads of children as he worked the crowd. Somebody mentioned the permit issue, and the mayor disappeared into his nearby office. Fifteen minutes later he emerged with a slip of paper and a megaphone. During a break in the caroling, he stepped out in front of the crowd.

"I've just been on the phone with Mr. Ottmeyer," he said into the megaphone. "And the town attorney wanted me to make a few things clear." Some scattered moans drifted forward. "First of all, the Town of Possum did not request this display, fund this display, or even know about this display. But he also reminded me that this is a town square, a quintessential public forum—" the mayor couldn't help but grin a little at the enormous word that Ottmeyer had given him—"and that we would be on shaky legal ground if we tried to keep Mr. Hammond from celebrating a national holiday with this peaceful little display of his. I've therefore taken it upon myself to grant him a permit to display his manger scene at all times between the hours of 6:00 p.m. and midnight from now until December 25."

Frumpkin turned and handed the paper to Thomas while the crowd cheered. Someone yelled for a speech as if they really expected Thomas to say something into the megaphone. Soon others joined in the chant, and Thomas realized that he had no choice.

He took the megaphone from the mayor. "Thanks," he said. "Thanks to all of y'all." Then he handed the megaphone back to the mayor, and the crowd roared wildly. Someone broke into a rendition of "We Wish You a Merry Christmas," and others followed along, though most mumbled through a fair amount of forgotten words. This led to another round of singing as more people continued to pour onto the square.

The crowd ebbed and the hot cider flowed for nearly three hours. People formed a line to come forward and pass before the straw manger. It seemed to Thomas that the Virgin Mary was smiling.

She continued to smile until nearly nine o'clock. "I reckon I better shut down for tonight," Thomas announced. The crowd had died down, and there was no longer a line. "I'll be back out here tomorrow night."

Vince Harrod stepped forward, huddled into his long overcoat as if he were some kind of secret agent who had been hiding in the crowd. He handed Thomas a typed piece of paper. Apparently his cell phone had been busy too. "I wouldn't be so sure about that," he said.

14

WEDNESDAY, DECEMBER 13

Theresa didn't wait for the alarm to go off at 5:30 before she crawled out of bed and padded to the kitchen. She hadn't been this tired since the first few colicky weeks of little Elizabeth's life—a nonstop screamfest that deprived Theresa of sleep and nearly her sanity. Last night she had been kept awake not by Elizabeth but by worries about today's court hearing and the way things were escalating out of control. Thomas, on the other hand, slept soundly, snoring as loud as ever. Twice she woke him up, supposedly to stop his snoring. "*Thomas*, can you roll over on your side, please?" Secretly she hoped he would wake up enough for them to discuss this situation.

But not Thomas. Stubborn, silent Thomas. He could sleep through Armageddon.

Theresa flipped on the kitchen light, emptied yesterday's coffee grinds from the filter, and started a new pot. She warmed Elizabeth's bottle just in case. She started cooking the oatmeal and dropped two slices of bread in the toaster. She heard the alarm go off in the bedroom and Thomas roll out of bed. Within minutes he had dressed and joined her in the kitchen.

During the spring, summer, and fall, Thomas had a steady lawn-care business taking care of the rich folks in Virginia Beach and Chesapeake. During the winter, Thomas morphed into a lumberjack, paying farmers for the right to cut trees on their property, then selling the firewood to convenience stores for resale to customers. He would be gone before the sun came up, spending his first few hours splitting and wrapping the logs he had hauled out to the road the prior day. Thomas could never understand why anybody would pay so much for a half-dozen fireplace logs. Based on the proven willingness of city folk to pay for bottled water and bundled wood, Thomas kept threatening to figure out a way to distribute clean country air as well. "I'll put it in aerosol cans and sell it in New York City," he said. "Before you know it, I'll be a billionaire."

Theresa spent the days cooped up in the trailer, taking care of Elizabeth and two other toddlers who belonged to a single working mom. The Hammonds weren't rich, but they got the bills paid. Their savings account, however, had been wiped out by medical bills and the funeral expenses for little Joshie, not quite a year and a half ago.

"Mornin'," Thomas said as he came over and kissed Theresa.

"Mornin'."

He ate in silence for a few minutes while Theresa put away the dishes that had been drying in the drainer overnight.

"Comin' to court this afternoon?" he asked.

"Don't think so."

Thomas paused as he took a sip of coffee and a bite of oatmeal. "'Cause?"

Theresa placed the final few glasses in the cupboard and hesitated. She wanted to support him so badly—but why did it always have to be *them*? Why couldn't somebody else fight this battle? It couldn't come at a worse time.

She sighed, lacking the emotional energy for a fight. She grabbed the peanut butter out of the cabinet, the jelly from the refrigerator, and started making sandwiches. "Elizabeth can't stay still that long. Plus I promised the other kids we'd go Christmas shopping after school."

"Already spent a lot of money on the plywood," Thomas said as if Theresa didn't know. "Don't get carried away."

"Forty-eight dollars for the plywood," Theresa said. "And another eighteen-fifty for the paint."

More silence followed, which drove Theresa crazy. "That's sixty-six dollars we don't have, Thomas."

He grunted and ate a few more bites of oatmeal. "I'll make it up this week. Firewood sales are always good around the holidays."

You gonna sell firewood from jail? she wanted to ask. But what good would that do? She should be supportive, not nagging. But sixty-six bucks was a lot of money. And that federal judge scared her. She fixed lunch in silence and thought about everything that could go wrong. She waited until he had finished his breakfast to bring it up again.

"What did Jasmine say?" Theresa asked. She put two PB&J sandwiches in small sandwich bags and then placed them in a larger white plastic bag. She threw in a PowerBar, the remainder of an opened bag of chips, an apple, and a napkin.

Thomas had been watching her pack his lunch from the breakfast table. He stood and placed his dishes in the sink. "What am I gonna eat for dessert?" he asked.

Theresa shook her head and placed a brownie in his lunch bag too. "Now, what did Jasmine say?"

"She thinks we've got a good case. Says the worst I'll get is a good chewing out."

"And then?"

"Then, in a worst-case scenario, the judge will tell me not to do it again."

"Then?"

Thomas picked up his lunch from the counter, added another brownie, and grabbed the drink cooler from the refrigerator. "We'll cross that bridge when we come to it."

Theresa came over and wrapped her arms around him. He put his lunch on the counter and gave her a quick hug, the same kind of out-the-door hug he gave her every morning. But this time she didn't let go. She had to say something, though she couldn't look at him when she did. "I can't go through this again, Thomas." Her voice became thick. "Promise me you won't go to jail again."

He held on to her and stroked the back of her hair. "I'm not going to jail, Theresa. Jasmine said we've got a good case."

"Promise me you'll back off if you have to."

He hesitated.

"Promise me, Thomas."

He kissed the top of her head and gave her a squeeze—a subtle signal that it was time to let go. "You know I can't do that, Theresa. A man's got to do what a man's got to do."

She *hated* that expression. *Hated* it! What's that even supposed to mean? That a man's got to go on some crusade for Christmas and ignore the needs of his own family?

She unwrapped her arms and pursed her lips. She had stood silently by her man so many times in the past. Thomas and his crusades. Thomas and his convictions. It had already cost them a son. Couldn't he see that? "Sometimes," she said, "a man's got to do what's right for his family."

Thomas just looked at her, sadness and resolve filling his eyes. Then he grabbed his lunch and headed for the door.

15

Tiger loved the Dollar Store! He squeezed the five-dollar bill in his right hand and elbowed his way from aisle to aisle, breathlessly checking out all the stuff. There were so many people in the store, he could barely move around. But fortunately Tiger was small and could squeeze past people and . . . whoops! He knocked over a bunch of Christmas tree decorations and some Christmas curly swirl. He bent over to pick up a box of the ornaments and took a quick look around—nobody watching. He gently kicked the stuff over to the side and took off. His mom always said if you broke something in a store, they made you pay for it. No way was he gonna use his money on Christmas curly swirl.

Halfway down the next aisle he found some stuff his

mommy would love! Bubble bath, necklaces, girlie junk everywhere! Stinky, Tiger's big sister, was hanging out in this aisle. Her real name was Hannah, a name she now wanted everyone to use, but Tiger liked the nickname his dad had given her when she was still in diapers. When Stinky saw Tiger, she put her hand over her little shopping basket, as if she had already picked out his present. Then she hurried off to another aisle.

Something caught his eye that he knew his mommy would like. "Excuse me," he said, pulling on the leg of a kind-looking lady. "Can you reach that for me?" He pointed to the necklace, and the lady smiled and handed it to him.

It looked even better up close. It was a big necklace with a flashing light on a little thing that hung down. If you twisted the top of that hangy-down thing, right where it attached to the necklace, the necklace would flash—like a police car. How cool!

Mom was done.

Dad was next, and Dad was hard. Tiger covered a few more rows and decided to be practical. White underwear. His dad could always use some more underwear. Tiger grabbed a pack and threw them into his little basket. Not the most exciting gift, but Dad already had everything he wanted. Dad's gift was history. Now for Lizzy. But what did you get for a baby?

Searching for the perfect gift, Tiger made his way down the toy aisle. This was unbelievable, so many things to choose from! His eyes bugged out as he surveyed the mountains of cool stuff. A plastic snake. Action figures and little race cars. Dinosaurs and lizards. Hey, that would be a good idea—a lizard for Lizzie. But then . . . oh, my goodness!

Tiger grabbed a package of two Wild West cowboy guns with rubber-tipped darts and everything. He thought about how much fun it would be, racing around the trailer, sneaking up on his dad. Bam! His dad would groan and stumble around and then fall down dead.

He raced around the store hunting for Stinky. "C'mere a minute," he said breathlessly.

He dragged her back to the toy aisle and pointed out the guns. "Those are really cool," he said.

She turned up her nose. "I don't like guns."

"Not for you, Stinky. I'm dus' saying, if you were wondering what to get for *me* . . ."

Stinky, who had been using her body to protect her basket from Tiger's efforts to peek, did not seem impressed. "Hannah, not Stinky," she scolded. "And I already got yours."

"But what if I don't like it?"

"I already showed Mom. She said you'll like it."

"I really like guns," Tiger said, leaning forward a little so he could sneak a look at what Stinky had in that basket.

"No peeking," Stinky said, twisting so he couldn't see. "'Sides, if I get you the guns, you'll know what I got you. And that will take all the fun out of it."

Shucks. At least he had tried. But Stinky was a girl. What did she know about guns?

Then another idea hit him. His dad weren't no girl. And his daddy loved guns. His dad had as much fun as Tiger when they played with guns.

After Stinky had disappeared around the end of the aisle, Tiger grabbed the guns and put them in his basket. Then he took out the underwear and, after checking for store clerks, placed them in the bin of plastic snakes.

Boy, his dad would love these guns. And as Tiger knew better than most, you can make a few pair of used underwear go a long way.

16

Even though Jasmine had another final less than one day away, she spent almost the entire morning and early afternoon on Wednesday preparing for the show-cause hearing. True to his threats, Vince Harrod had filed the paperwork necessary to drag both the Town of Possum and Thomas Hammond back into court to answer for their conduct the night before. Because Ichabod already had a full docket on Wednesday, the hearing was not scheduled to begin until four in the afternoon.

This time Thomas was a party and Jasmine was an attorney of record, with Arnold Ottmeyer serving as her supervising attorney. She sat at the defendant's table with Ottmeyer, Mayor Frumpkin, and Thomas. Harrod, representing himself as a citizen of the Commonwealth of Virginia, sat alone at the plaintiff's table.

The short notice for the hearing didn't seem to detract from attendance. More than half the seats were full, mostly with representatives of the media. A half hour before the hearing, the media satellite trucks had rolled into position.

Jasmine straightened the pile of papers in front of her. Final exams were one thing, Ichabod quite another. She knew that Ichabod would come out swinging, especially if she'd seen the morning paper. "Possum Resident Flaunts Court Order," the headline read.

But Jasmine did have one thing going for her—an opinion by the U.S. Supreme Court—*Capital Square Review and Advisory Board v. Pinette*. She had read the case four times already. It was probably the only thing standing between her client and contempt.

"All rise! The Honorable Cynthia Baker-Kline presiding."

Ichabod began the proceedings by reminding everyone of the procedural posture of the case, probably for the benefit of the press. She reiterated her prior ruling, then explained that Harrod had filed a motion seeking sanctions against the Town of Possum, Mayor Frumpkin, and Thomas Hammond for violating her prior order. As a result, Ichabod had scheduled this show-cause hearing—an opportunity for the defendants to "show cause" why they shouldn't be held in contempt.

"I'll hear from Mr. Hammond's counsel first," Ichabod announced, "since he seems to be the person who started this uproar."

Jasmine stood and walked to the lectern. "May it please the court, my name is Jasmine Woodfaulk and I represent—"

"Yes, yes, I'm aware of all that," Ichabod snapped. "Did

your client erect a manger scene on the Possum town square last night in direct violation of this court's order?"

"Yes and no," Jasmine replied. "Yes, my client erected a crèche on the town square. But no, he didn't violate the court's order."

"I understand the yes part," Ichabod fired back. "But you'd better explain the no part . . . and you'd better make it good."

"This court's order forbade the town, or any agents of the town, from erecting a crèche on the town square because it might be seen as an unconstitutional endorsement of religion. But as the court knows, the First Amendment's establishment clause applies only to governmental bodies, not private individuals. Last night Thomas Hammond acted as a private individual. The only thing the town did was to grant him access to a traditional public forum—the town square. Accordingly, the controlling case is the Supreme Court case of *Capitol Square Review v. Pinette* . . ." Jasmine picked up some copies from her counsel table, handing one to the court clerk and one to Harrod. "Under *Pinette*, the town can't keep someone like Thomas from erecting a manger scene on property traditionally open for speech and demonstrations, or it violates his free-speech rights."

The clerk handed Ichabod a copy of the case, but the judge set it aside. "I'm familiar with *Pinette*," she said. "The Klan wanted to erect a cross on a state-owned plaza in Columbus, Ohio, that had been used for public speeches, gatherings, and festivals for more than a hundred years. But the *Pinette* case involved a political display. This display is purely religious, thereby implicating the establishment clause and requiring this court to be more circumspect about allowing it."

Jasmine felt a rush of adrenaline. The judge couldn't have been more wrong. "With all due respect, Your Honor, that's precisely the argument the Supreme Court rejected in *Pinette*. Listen to what Justice Scalia said, writing for the majority . . ." Jasmine picked up the case and went straight to her favorite quote. "The Klan's 'religious display in Capitol Square was private expression' and, 'far from being a First Amendment orphan, was as fully protected under the Free Speech Clause as secular private expression. Indeed, in Anglo American history, at least, government suppression of speech has been so commonly directed *precisely* at religious speech that a free-speech clause without religion would be *Hamlet* without the prince.'"

Jasmine looked up from the case and measured the expression on Ichabod's face. The judge did not look pleased, but she didn't say anything either; she just scribbled some notes. "Not only that," Jasmine said, "but Justice Scalia had a few words to say about the argument that religious speech should be entitled to less protection than other speech, much the same way that pornography is entitled to less protection." She quickly found the other quote she had highlighted. "'It will be a sad day when this court casts piety in with pornography and finds the First Amendment more hospitable to private expletives than to private prayers. This would be merely bizarre—'"

"Enough," Ichabod interrupted. "I get the point." She turned to Harrod. "It seems to me that if the Klan can do it, Mr. Hammond is certainly entitled."

Harrod rose confidently to his feet. "Before Ms. Woodfaulk graduates from law school, I hope she will learn to read the concurring opinions as well as the majority opinions for critical Supreme Court cases."

Jasmine bristled. Why did Harrod always have to make it so personal?

"As Justice O'Connor points out in her concurrence, Capitol Square had traditionally been open to a wide variety of displays, the Klan used the same permit process as everyone else, and the display was to include a sign indicating it was not sponsored by the city. We intend to prove that all of those factors cut the other way in this case."

"Just a moment," Ichabod said. She picked up the *Pinette* case and read it carefully, page by page, as the lawyers and spectators watched in respectful silence. When she finished, she took off her reading glasses, closed her eyes, and pinched the bridge of her nose as if this whole affair was giving her a migraine. Then she slipped the glasses back on the end of her nose and glanced over them at Harrod. "Counsel, at this stage, I'm inclined to agree with Ms. Woodfaulk. So why don't you call your first witness?"

"Mayor Bert Frumpkin," Harrod said without hesitation.

17

HARROD RACED THROUGH a few preliminary questions and then got right to the point.

"At the time Mr. Hammond erected his manger scene on the town square last night, did he have a permit?"

"Not when he erected it. But before the night was over—he did."

Harrod stepped out from behind the lectern and moved a little closer to the witness.

"In my courtroom," Ichabod boomed, "attorneys stay behind the lectern."

Jasmine wished she had a picture of the surprised look on Harrod's face. It was a whose-side-are-you-on-anyway? look.

"Yes, Your Honor," Harrod said, retreating. Then to the witness: "Who issued the permit?"

"I did."

"Does the mayor normally issue permits for displays in the town of Possum?"

Frumpkin rubbed his hands together and thought about this for a moment. "Not usually. Most of the time the entire town council votes on permits for things like parades and such. So no, I wouldn't say I normally issue permits myself."

"When's the last time you issued a permit by yourself, prior to last night?"

More thinking by Frumpkin, this time accompanied by a mustache twirl. "Never."

"I see. And why didn't the town council vote on Mr. Hammond's display?"

"Because we didn't have time. Mr. Hammond had already set up his manger scene on the town square. We either had to give him a permit or declare him a trespasser and have him arrested." Frumpkin looked at Thomas. "We weren't going to arrest someone for celebrating Christmas."

Jasmine glanced to Ichabod, but the judge had her game face on.

"So, if necessary, you as the mayor can grant permits without a vote of the council?"

"That's what I did."

"Earlier today, did you as town mayor receive a request for a permit that I filed for a demonstration on the town square? I'm referring now to the Saturnalia Festival request for December 17–24, the weeklong party to end all parties in honor of Saturn, god of peace and plenty."

Frumpkin scoffed. "I received it."

"Did you reject it?"

"Of course."

"On what basis?"

Frumpkin looked at Ottmeyer as if they had practiced this answer many times. "First of all, I had a concern about disorderly conduct. Second, it seemed that the sponsor—meaning you—probably intended to serve alcohol and didn't have an alcohol permit. And third, I don't know of any town residents who worship Saturn, so I didn't think it would serve the citizens."

"Those are some interesting factors," Harrod said. "Are those types of guidelines written down someplace so that folks like me can make sure we comply with them in our requests?"

This brought another look from Frumpkin to Ottmeyer as if the attorney was supposed to have thought of this question as well. "Not that I'm aware of."

"So then, it's just totally up to you as the mayor, and you base that decision in part on how many adherents to that religion you believe live in Possum?"

The mayor swallowed and twitched. *Just answer the question!* Jasmine wanted to say. *It only makes it worse when you squirm around.*

"I guess that's about right," he finally said.

Harrod was smart enough to let the silence hang out there for a moment. He made a note on his legal pad. Ichabod made a note on her pad. And Jasmine made one on her pad: *Talk Mom into running for mayor.*

"Mr. Harrod?" Ichabod prompted.

"Sorry, Your Honor. Now did you consider a second permit request from me today as well?"

Frumpkin answered tentatively, "Yes."

"On behalf of?"

"Well, the written application you filed said it was on behalf of the Gay and Lesbian Alliance of Hampton Roads . . . or something to that effect."

"You've got a good memory," Harrod said. "What kind of event was this group requesting?"

Frumpkin shook his head in disgust. "They called it a 'We Wish You a Merry Christmas Fashion Show.'"

"And the purpose of the event?"

"Well, again, according to what you wrote, it was to show the straight folk in Possum what the song means when it says, 'Don we now our gay apparel.'"

"Did you grant the permit?"

To this, Frumpkin just snorted.

"I take it that means no."

"Yes, that means no."

"Why not?"

Frumpkin didn't bother looking at his attorney this time, apparently confident that he could handle this on his own. "Well, first, that's a total misunderstanding of the song. That line means 'happy' apparel, not 'gay' apparel as we think of it today. But second, and more important, I've seen the way gays dress at these things—Speedos, leather necklaces, body piercings—all that junk. Your permit even came with a picture of a gay man in a Speedo and a Santa Claus hat. No way I'm permitting that on the town square."

"Because?"

"Well, first of all, it's a public health hazard—these gay guys will all catch pneumonia . . ."

Ichabod snickered loud enough to be heard over her mike.

"And second, it's just indecent. Can't have our Possum kids exposed to that nonsense."

Harrod flipped his pen a few times. "So you not only determine which religious groups can display based in part on how many adherents they have, but you also determine whether or not other groups can display based on how decent or indecent you think their message is?"

"Yes."

"And the Ku Klux Klan, Mr. Frumpkin—is their message decent or indecent?"

"Indecent."

"So if they applied for a permit for the Possum town square, you wouldn't give them one?"

"Absolutely not."

Next to Jasmine, Ottmeyer placed his left hand on his forehead and wrote a quick note with his right. He passed it to Jasmine. *Any ideas?*

He's your witness, Jasmine wrote back.

Forty-five minutes later Ichabod issued her ruling.

"Based on the testimony, it is painfully clear to this court that the permit process in Possum is a far cry from the type of fair and nondiscriminatory procedure that was employed in the *Pinette* case. In Possum, the mayor basically decides which displays he likes and which displays he doesn't like based on his personal and subjective opinion. This hardly creates the kind of open public forum where it would violate the free-speech rights of Mr. Hammond if he were not allowed to display his crèche."

At this, Ichabod took off her reading glasses and glared at

the defense table. "Mr. Hammond and Mr. Frumpkin, you've now had your fun at this court's expense. Because you had at least some hope of justifying your conduct based on the *Pinette* case cited by Ms. Woodfaulk, I'm not going to hold you in contempt today. But let me make one thing perfectly clear. Mr. Hammond, if you display any more manger scenes on the town square, or, Mr. Frumpkin, if you authorize, permit, or sanction any such scenes erected by Mr. Hammond or any other person . . . then I will hold you gentlemen in contempt of court and you could be spending the holidays in jail. Am I making myself clear?"

"Yes, Your Honor," Frumpkin said.

Jasmine could just about feel the heat coming from Thomas.

"Mr. Hammond?" Ichabod said.

"Crystal clear, Your Honor."

At that, Ichabod banged her gavel. "Court adjourned."

It took Thomas less than three hours to make it home, load up Bebo and the wooden Mary, the shepherd, and the animals, and set up his manger scene in the Possum town square.

This time, as the crowd gathered and the apple cider flowed, Joseph was not smiling.

18

Jasmine felt the vibration and checked her phone. *Thomas Hammond (home).* She ignored it. Whatever he needed could wait. Jasmine was in the law school library, studying furiously for her UCC exam, trying to make up for the time she had lost that morning.

You didn't bluff your way through the Uniform Commercial Code.

The phone vibrated again. Same number. This time she hit the Power button and turned it off. She focused on the types of disclaimers needed to negate an implied warranty of merchantability. She memorized the magic words needed. She took note of the font size. But her mind wandered to the words of Professor Arnold from the first day of the legal aid clinic: *"By signing up for this course, you are making a commitment to treat your legal aid clients with the same respect and dignity you will give your most important clients when you begin practicing law. Being a professional means your commitment to the client doesn't change based on the client's wealth or status."*

Jasmine sighed and slipped out of the library to return the call. Theresa answered on the first ring.

"Thank God," she said when Jasmine identified herself. "Jasmine, I know you're in the middle of exams and I hated to even call. But honestly . . ." The words seemed to catch in Theresa's throat and the phone went silent.

"What is it?" Jasmine asked.

"I just didn't know what else to do." The words came pouring out. "Thomas is back on the town square with his manger scene. I tried to stop him, but he wouldn't listen. Jasmine, could you . . . could you possibly talk to him?"

Jasmine hesitated, calculating how much she still had to cover and how little time she had to do it. Without any breaks at all, she might be able to get three or four hours' sleep tonight. But if she drove to Possum?

"Does anybody you know have a cell phone at the square?"

Silence. "I'm sure somebody does, Jasmine. But you've got to know Thomas. I don't think a phone call would work."

"How long has he been out there?"

"Maybe half an hour."

Jasmine blew out a hard breath to signal her frustration. But then she thought about the fury of Ichabod and the little Hammond children. Somebody had to get Thomas away from the square. "Okay, Theresa. I'll go talk to him."

"Thank you *so* much!" Theresa sounded on the verge

of tears, and Jasmine didn't waste any time getting off the phone.

Forty-five minutes later Jasmine parallel parked on Main Street, Possum, in the closest place she could find to the square. She still had to walk nearly a block. As she approached, she heard the voices and saw the crowd singing by candlelight. Instead of the boisterous activity that Jasmine had experienced on Saturday, she felt a reverence here, the words of "Silent Night" drifting upward.

Someone handed Jasmine a candle with a slip of cardboard around the bottom to protect her hand from wax drippings. A candle was held toward hers to light it. Straining her neck, Jasmine looked over heads toward the manger scene, where Thomas stood still as a rock. Jasmine lingered there at the back of the crowd for a moment and hummed along, the words from the second and third verses of "Silent Night" eluding her as surely as sections of the UCC would tomorrow. Someone with a steaming cup of something leaned next to her. "If you want some hot apple cider, it's over there," he whispered. "They aren't charging for it tonight."

"Thanks. I'm good."

She stayed for "O Little Town of Bethlehem" and the first verse of "Joy to the World." Then she blew out her candle, joined a few others who were slipping away from the crowd, and headed back into the darkness.

★

Jasmine started to dial Theresa's number three or four times on the way back to the law school but each time talked herself out of it. What would she tell her anyway? *Hey, Theresa, it's Jasmine. I just drove out to the town square and sang along with a few Christmas carols. Thomas is fine, though he'll probably be in jail tomorrow.*

But what could Jasmine have done? tell the crowd to stop celebrating Christmas? scold Thomas like a schoolchild in front of the whole village? Even if she did, she knew Thomas wouldn't listen. She wasn't sure what she had expected to accomplish when she got to the town square, but she definitely hadn't been expecting the kind of worship experience she found. There were some things you just didn't interrupt—like standing up in the middle of a prayer meeting at church and asking if anyone knows where the bathroom is. This had been that type of occasion.

As she wound through the swamps that separated the countryside surrounding Possum from the city of Virginia Beach, Jasmine thought about the challenges swirling around her. A UCC exam she wasn't prepared for. A client about to get hammered by a federal court judge. Her little sister's basketball team being coached by a Bobby Knight wannabe. At least she had her offer with Gold, Franks. A bright note among the discordant din that had become her life.

Her cell phone rang with the song she had just programmed in last weekend—"We Wish You a Merry Christmas." How ironic was that? She looked down, expecting to see the cell number of one of her law school buddies or maybe Theresa Hammond calling, but it was a number she didn't recognize.

"Hello?"

"Does your client have a death wish?"

It was a familiar male voice—strident, angry. "Who's this?"

"Vince Harrod. Have you heard what that lunatic is doing tonight?"

"Let me guess. Standing on the town square dressed like Joseph while Possumites hold candles and sing Christmas carols?"

"You've been out there?"

"A lucky guess."

"Listen, Jasmine, this is serious. I can't just sit back while he thumbs his nose at the judge's order."

"Why not? You've already made your point. He's not hurting anybody."

"Are you serious? He's violating the Constitution! He's ignoring a federal court judge! He thinks he's above the law!"

Jasmine really wanted to tell this guy off, but Harrod held all the cards. Still, it wouldn't hurt to yank his chain a little. "So serve him with another subpoena. You know where he is."

"I'm not going out there. People in Possum have guns, and they're getting sick of me. Besides, I don't have to serve him again since he's now a party to a pending lawsuit. I just have to notify you as his attorney that I'm going to call the clerk's office first thing in the morning and ask for a ten o'clock hearing."

Great. Right in the middle of my UCC exam.

"You can't do that, Vince." Jasmine tried to sound like a seasoned litigator, calling Harrod by his first name. "I've got a final from nine until noon."

Harrod laughed out loud. "I'm not used to scheduling around someone's law school exams," he said. "How about one o'clock?"

"How 'bout I just talk to my client and get him to agree not to go out there again."

"One o'clock it is," Vince responded. "Let your client know."

"Merry Christmas," Jasmine said.

"Happy holidays," Vince said.

They hung up and Jasmine dialed Theresa's number.

Theresa answered on the first ring. "Hello."

"I'm afraid I've got some bad news," Jasmine said.

19

Jasmine struggled through her UCC exam, living proof that you should never take an arduous test on just two hours' sleep. So much for second in her class.

Thirty-five minutes later, exhausted and hungry, she was driving around downtown Norfolk near the federal courthouse, looking for a parking spot. The place was a madhouse. *They can't all be here because of our case. Can they?*

She gave up looking for a spot near the courthouse and entered the parking deck for the MacArthur mall. This turned out to be another mistake, since the Christmas shoppers were out in force, and it took Jasmine nearly ten more minutes to find a spot.

She threw her backpack over her shoulder and raced toward the courthouse. The backpack would scream "law student," but what could she do? She had too much stuff to just throw it in a file folder like she had yesterday. She had been intending to buy a briefcase these past few days, but when did she have time?

At least it wasn't raining, though the gusting wind was probably frizzing her hair big-time.

She turned the corner onto the sidewalk in front of the courthouse at about five minutes before one o'clock and nearly stopped in her tracks. The place was lined with camera trucks and news reporters. NBC. ABC. CBS. Fox News. CNN. Throughout law school she had dreamed of a high-profile case like this. But in her dreams she always had a brilliant legal argument or at least a good defense. Today she had nothing. She would have to throw her client on the mercy of the court while the entire nation watched.

Jasmine ignored the shouted questions as she elbowed her way into the courthouse. Once there, she waited her turn at the metal detector.

"Briefcases and overcoats on the belt," the federal marshal said mechanically. He noticed Jasmine. "Backpacks, too."

A few minutes later Jasmine checked her watch as she slipped into the seat next to Thomas. One o'clock on the nose. Ichabod still hadn't taken the bench.

She leaned next to the big man so that Ottmeyer and Frumpkin, seated on her right, wouldn't hear. "Here's the drill," Jasmine whispered. "I apologize first. Then you promise to abide by the court's order in the future. Then I'll argue for mercy based on the fact that you've got a family to support. Our goal today is to avoid jail time. Got it?"

Thomas looked down at the table and frowned. "I can't promise not to go out there again, Ms. Woodfaulk."

Jasmine felt her neck muscles tighten and leaned closer to him. She didn't have time for this—Ichabod would be on the bench any minute! "Thomas, you don't have a choice here. She's a federal judge. She has the power to keep you off that square. The only issue is whether she does it by throwing you in jail or whether you agree to do it voluntarily. Do you understand?"

"Oh, I understand. It's just—"

"Order in the court," the clerk cried. "The Honorable Cynthia Baker-Kline now presiding."

Ichabod gaveled the court into session—"Remain seated"—and stared at Thomas. To his credit, Thomas kept his gaze on the table. Ichabod then turned her icy gaze to Frumpkin.

"Mayor Frumpkin, I understand that Mr. Hammond set up a manger display on the town square last night. Was this display pursuant to a town permit or any other form of permission from the town?"

Jasmine looked at Frumpkin and thought the little man was trembling. "No, Your Honor."

She turned to Harrod. "Do you have any evidence to the contrary?"

"No, Your Honor."

She returned her ire to Thomas, and her pulsing neck vein picked up tempo. "Mr. Hammond, what do you have to say for yourself?"

Jasmine stood on weak knees. "Your Honor, Mr. Hammond would like to apologize to the court—"

"*Sit down*, Ms. Woodfaulk."

Jasmine had never seen or heard of such a thing. A lawyer not even allowed to argue for her client? "But, Your Honor—"

"Sit down."

Jasmine scowled and took her seat. She shook her head a little to show how ridiculous this was.

"You'll get your turn to argue the case," Ichabod snapped. "But first, I want to hear from your client by way of testimony." Again she glared at Thomas. "Now, Mr. Hammond, what do you have to say for yourself?"

Thomas hesitated, then rose to his feet.

Should I tell him to plead the Fifth? Jasmine wondered. *Can you even do that when you're facing contempt of court, rather than an actual criminal charge?* This whole scenario was so far outside anything Jasmine had studied in law school. Thomas hadn't even been sworn in.

Thomas drew a deep breath and faced the court. "With all due respect, Your Honor, I answer to a higher power."

Jasmine shifted in her seat. *What would Johnnie Cochran have done in a situation like this? What would Professor Arnold do?*

"Did you set up a manger scene on the Possum town square last night in direct violation of my order?"

Jasmine jumped up. "Don't answer that."

Ichabod turned on her. "What?"

"I'm instructing my client not to answer on the grounds that it might incriminate him."

"Brilliant, Counsel." Ichabod shook her head to show how stupid the tactic was. Then she turned to Mayor Frumpkin. "Did you go out to the town square last night?"

"Yes." Frumpkin's voice was so soft that Jasmine could barely hear it.

"Did Mr. Hammond set up a manger scene on the town square in direct violation of my order?"

"Yes."

"Thank you, Mr. Frumpkin."

Now Jasmine felt like a complete idiot. She had angered the judge for no apparent reason.

Ichabod turned back to Thomas. "Do you intend to go out there and set it up again tonight?" she asked.

"Yes."

"Have a seat." Ichabod tilted her head and gave Jasmine a nod. "You may argue now, Counsel."

For five minutes Jasmine talked about Thomas and his family. She spoke of the American tradition of civil disobedience. She invoked Martin Luther King, Harriet Tubman, and Rosa Parks. She asked Ichabod to issue a stay of her ruling so that Jasmine could appeal to the Fourth Circuit and get a final word before Ichabod did something so drastic as send a man to jail. All the while Ichabod listened attentively, her eyes drilling holes in each of Jasmine's arguments.

When Jasmine finished, Harrod jumped up. "May I respond, Your Honor?"

"That won't be necessary," Ichabod said. "The court finds the analogies to the civil rights protestors most inappropriate, especially since my colleagues on this very court, the Eastern District of Virginia sitting in Norfolk, paid such a high price for their courageous rulings against segregation at a time when it was most unpopular for them to take that stand. If anything, your client is more analogous to Judge Roy Moore, and we all know how that turned out."

Ichabod's nose flared a few times as she considered her options. "Mr. Hammond, please stand." Jasmine stood with him. "You may believe that you are subject to a higher authority, but you must learn that you are also subject to *my* authority. Though I am reluctant to take this step, your conduct leaves me no other recourse. I am hereby finding you in contempt of court and sentencing you to twenty-four hours in a federal holding cell. But I'm also putting you on notice right now, Mr. Hammond. Any further violations of my order after your release will result in a much longer sentence." She paused, letting the gravity of her words sink in. "Am I making myself clear?"

"Crystal clear, Your Honor."

Jasmine had heard that before.

20

LATER THAT AFTERNOON Jasmine received a call with a 212 area code. New York City. She tried not to sound nervous. "Hello."

"Jazz, this is Pearson."

"Hey, Mr. Payne."

"Call me Pearson, please."

"Okay, Pearson." *Man, that sounded strange.* "What's up?"

"You're making quite a name for yourself down there, Jazz. You been watching CNN?"

Should she tell him she preferred Fox News? "No. Why?"

"They've been running that story about the Possum manger scene every fifteen minutes or so. My partners are starting to talk."

117

"Is that a problem?" She sensed that it was.

"Well, let's put it this way: Possum is not exactly coming off as the center of enlightenment here. And your involvement on the side of the religious Right has some of my partners concerned. Heck, most of 'em haven't been inside a church since their kids got married." Pearson hesitated. Jasmine decided to wait him out. "I'm going to bat for you, Jazz, but help me out by keeping a low profile. These guys are afraid that word will leak out about your coming to Gold, Franks, and the New York press would have a field day."

Jasmine wasn't sure what to say. In truth, she had already been thinking about withdrawing from the case. How could she represent a client who wouldn't take her advice? But on the other hand, she didn't like being pressured by a firm she didn't even work for yet.

"Thanks for your support, Pearson. But I don't understand why your partners don't side with the First Amendment on this one."

Pearson chuckled. "Not my partners. They're on the side of billing clients. And they don't want this case to impact our hard-earned reputation with our decidedly liberal client base."

"I understand," Jasmine said, though the idealist in her didn't understand at all. "And I'll govern myself accordingly."

"You're going to fit in just fine at Gold, Franks," Pearson said. "And don't worry. I've got your back."

That evening, in a grungy visitation booth at the federal holding cell, both Theresa and Jasmine tried to extract a pledge from Thomas that he would not set up another manger scene after his release.

Theresa approached it from a mother's perspective, begging Thomas to consider the impact on their children. She told Thomas how Hannah had cried when she learned her daddy would be in jail. "Tiger stuck up for you, blaming the judge," Theresa said. "I told them both you were a hero, but all they could think about was the time you spent in prison when Joshie died—and how the court took them away from me for a few weeks."

When Thomas didn't respond, Jasmine started in. "You've made your stand, Thomas, and we'll appeal Judge Baker-Kline's rulings. We've got a good shot at getting her overturned in the Fourth Circuit and making some good law. But I can't defend someone who blatantly disregards the court's orders in the meantime. And I won't represent someone who doesn't follow my legal advice."

"Listen to her, Thomas," Theresa said. "The judge may not be so lenient next time."

But Thomas set his jaw. "I love you, Theresa," he said. "And, Jasmine, you've done good. But if you gotta drop the case, I understand." Thomas stared at his hands, fingers laced together on the table in front of him. "But somebody's gotta take a stand. Somebody's gotta say 'enough is enough,' or everything our country stands for goes right down the toilet. And right now I don't see nobody else willin' to do it."

Thomas made eye contact with his wife. "I'm sorry, but this ain't over."

Jasmine handed Thomas a one-page legal document—her motion to withdraw as counsel of record. "Then I'll be filing this tomorrow," she said. "I need you to sign it."

Instead of pleading for her to stay on the case, Thomas just nodded. He signed the document with the pen Jasmine provided. "Thanks for everything you've done."

This was harder than Jasmine thought it would be, especially when she saw the tears welling up in Theresa's eyes. "Can I have a couple of minutes alone with him?" Theresa asked.

21

The next morning Jasmine filed her motion to withdraw when the clerk's office opened at nine and obtained a hearing for eleven. She spent the time in between fighting the crowds at the MacArthur mall, though she didn't actually buy any presents. Despite the Christmas music and decorations, she found it hard to summon any Christmas spirit in light of the fact that she would be abandoning Thomas's case that day. She had developed a grudging respect for the man, despite the stubborn streak that made him impossible to defend.

The hearing went about as expected, with Thomas voicing no objection. Harrod was nice enough, telling Jasmine before the hearing that she had done excellent work "for a law student." A few members of the press attended, though Jasmine didn't give them any comment. She intended to keep her promise to Pearson Payne and maintain a low profile.

Ichabod didn't ask one question during the hearing. Professor Arnold had counseled Jasmine well, so she simply cited "irreconcilable differences between counsel and Mr. Hammond." This could cover any range of things and therefore wouldn't necessarily signal to the court that Jasmine was withdrawing because Thomas wouldn't listen to her advice about following court orders. The phrase—and the feeling in the pit of her stomach—made this feel more like a divorce than a simple conflict between a lawyer and client.

When Jasmine finished, Ichabod provided another of her vintage surprises. "I'm granting the motion," she said, "effective twenty-four hours from now, at twelve noon on Saturday. That will give Mr. Hammond sufficient time to find new counsel."

Jasmine balked at the ruling. It meant that she would still be representing Thomas when he got out of jail that afternoon. She suspected that Ichabod knew exactly what was going on between client and lawyer and wanted Jasmine to still be counsel of record on Friday night, advising Thomas against setting up his manger scene on the town square.

"Ms. Woodfaulk, I'd like to see you in my chambers for a few minutes," Ichabod announced. She turned to Harrod. "The court typically doesn't hold *ex parte* conferences," Ichabod said, referring to a meeting with one lawyer in the absence of the other, "but this is about Ms. Woodfaulk's motion to withdraw, not the merits of the case."

"That's fine, Your Honor," Harrod said.

A few minutes later Jasmine found herself ushered into

the vast expanse that was Ichabod's office. High ceilings, cathedral-style windows, luxurious velvet drapes, and an ornately carved mahogany desk all served as testaments to Ichabod's imperialistic power.

"Come in," Ichabod said, motioning to a chair in front of her desk. She took off her reading glasses and studied Jasmine the way opposing coaches used to look her over during warm-ups.

"Why are you really withdrawing?" the judge asked.

Better be careful here. "Off the record?"

Ichabod nodded.

"Because my client won't follow my advice."

Ichabod waited for a few beats. "If you're telling him to obey my orders, then you're giving him good advice."

Jasmine nodded. "I know."

Ichabod relaxed and leaned back in her chair. "You think I like putting your client in jail?"

Jasmine scrunched up her face, trying hard to read this enigmatic judge. "No, Your Honor."

"Look, I like Christmas just as much as your client, despite what the papers are saying. It's just that I also happen to value our Constitution, and particularly the separation of church and state that it requires, even more than I do your client's right to set up a manger scene on public property."

"I understand, Your Honor."

"Frankly, I don't think you do. But that's beside the point. Our country needs this issue settled, and I know the final word won't come from me. One way or another, this case is going to be appealed. And I don't like being reversed, Jasmine—" Ichabod penetrated Jasmine with a look as she said this—"but I also want to see a fair fight. You don't usually get good rulings when one side has bad lawyering."

Jasmine wasn't sure where this was headed. *Is she accusing me of bad lawyering?*

As if reading Jasmine's mind, the judge grinned. "Not you, Jasmine. That's my whole point. You're the *only* lawyer on your side who seems to know the law and cares enough to make the arguments that need to be made. For a law school student, you've done an admirable job."

Ichabod hesitated again, and Jasmine basked for a moment in the glow of the compliment.

"If you withdraw, you leave Mr. Hammond with what? a court-appointed lawyer? What if he refuses a court-appointed lawyer—which, knowing your client, he just might do. Then he proceeds *pro se*." Ichabod shook her head. "There's nothing worse than an out-of-control defendant proceeding *pro se*. The press gives him all kinds of sympathy, and he turns my courtroom into a circus."

"I hear you, Judge. But how can I represent someone who doesn't take my advice?"

"Get used to it," Ichabod scoffed. "If clients always followed their lawyer's advice, we wouldn't have any repeat offenders. Criminal defense lawyers make a killing off clients who ignore their advice. Comes with the territory."

That's why I'm not going to be a criminal defense lawyer, Jasmine wanted to say. But there was no sense arguing with Ichabod. "You're asking me to stay on?"

"Yes. It's why I made my order effective twenty-four hours from now. Gives you a chance to reconsider your motion if you want." The judge leaned forward. "I followed your basketball career when you played for Old Dominion, and I know you're not a quitter on the basketball court. I'm betting you're not a quitter in the courtroom, either."

This is so unfair. "Okay, Your Honor," Jasmine forced herself to say. "I'll think about it."

"You do that," Ichabod said. "But don't think that if you decide to stay on, I owe you any favors. You and your client are wrong about this. And my rulings will be sustained by the Fourth Circuit . . . after a fair fight, of course."

"Of course," Jasmine said. She left the judge's chambers feeling a little more proud and a lot more confused. *How did I get myself into this mess?*

22

He showed up at the trailer on Friday afternoon, and Theresa knew immediately that he was an answer to prayer. For one thing, she had been praying at the precise moment he knocked on her trailer door. Not the kind of quiet, kneeling-in-solitude prayer that she needed but seldom experienced anymore. But she *had* been praying, even as she amused three toddlers and listened to VeggieTales blaring in the background.

At first she hesitated to answer, thinking that he might be one of the reporters who had been seeking an interview. But when she peeked through one of the miniblinds and saw the big silver Cadillac, she knew he was some kind of angel, rather than a member of the demonic press.

Turned out that David A. Arginot III was a lawyer, but

then angels had been known to disguise themselves as some pretty unlikely characters. Why not a lawyer?

The impeccably dressed man handed Theresa a business card. "I am chief counsel for the Freddie Hester Evangelistic Association," he said, chest puffed out. The card was embossed in gold. "Reverend Hester himself sent me because he believes so strongly in what your husband is doing. May I come in and have a word with you?"

Theresa thought about what a mess her trailer was. There were toys strewn everywhere, with Elizabeth and another toddler crawling underfoot and a third child sitting in an automatic baby swing. But wasn't there a Scripture some-place that talked about always being hospitable because one might be entertaining angels unaware?

"Please come in," Theresa said, blushing a little. "But pardon the mess—I've just been so busy." She picked her way to the couch, moving a few toys and picking up some stray Cheerios so her new friend could sit down.

Mr. Arginot smiled, pressing his perfect mustache into his round puffy cheeks. "Don't worry about it; I've seen much worse." For some reason Theresa doubted it.

Her visitor crossed his legs and wrapped his hands around a knee. "I know that your lawyer filed a motion to withdraw today," he began. "And Reverend Hester wants to make sure you have good legal representation. He believes this case is a key battle in the cultural war for the soul of America."

Theresa simply nodded, amazed at how quickly this man had learned of Jasmine's withdrawal and then found Theresa's trailer. And the man was probably coming from . . . where? Florida? Wasn't that where Hester's ministry was located? It almost qualified as miraculous.

"In fact, Reverend Hester feels so strongly about this that he has already started a legal defense fund for your husband." At this revelation, gratitude surged through Theresa. And Arginot was not even finished.

"And I am willing to drop everything I'm doing right now and make myself available to personally serve as your husband's lawyer."

Elizabeth chose that precise moment to bump her head on the end of the couch and begin fussing. Theresa picked her up, kissed the spot, and began shushing the little girl. "I'm . . . I'm not sure what to say," Theresa stammered once Elizabeth had calmed down. It seemed too good to be true— a real lawyer, a Christian to boot, willing to take her case. And someone else was paying for it! "I mean, I . . . I can't believe you would do this . . . I was just praying . . . I'm a little overwhelmed."

This brought another reassuring smile from Arginot. No teeth should shine that brightly. He reached into his suit-coat pocket and withdrew a few sheets of paper and a pen. "I've taken the liberty of drafting a contract," he said. "You'll notice in the first paragraph that it specifies that all legal bills will be paid from the legal fund established by Reverend Hester."

Theresa gently placed Elizabeth back on the floor and the child motored off. She took the paper from Mr. Arginot and perused the first few paragraphs, just enough to realize she couldn't understand a word of it.

"Thomas will be released in a few hours," Arginot said confidently as if he had the case file memorized and knew everything there was to know about Theresa's family. "If it's okay with you, we'll pick him up at the jail together and let him know that he's in good legal hands." A broad smile. "Mine."

Theresa nodded.

"If he decides to retain me—at no cost, of course—you and the older kids will go from there to the Norfolk municipal airport, where we have a charter jet waiting to take you to New York. I will accompany Thomas back to Possum so he can resurrect the manger scene." Arginot looked around at the chaos. "You might want to get somebody to take care of your younger child tomorrow—this could be a whirlwind trip."

A babysitter? New York? Resurrect the manger scene? Who said anything about resurrecting the manger scene?

"New York?" she asked. One issue at a time.

"You'll be joining Reverend Hester, who's flying in from Orlando for a crusade in Madison Square Garden. Part of the problem with the way your case has been handled—and I don't want to sound critical of your lawyer; she's doing a good job for a law student—but part of the challenge is that we're losing the publicity war. We've got to get your story out there. And Reverend Hester is making tentative arrangements, even as we speak, for some joint appearances for you, the kids, and him on some Saturday morning wake-up shows."

Television? Theresa broke into a cold sweat just thinking about it. "But I don't really want to go on—"

"Excuse me," Arginot interrupted as he reached for a vibrating blue doohickey clipped to his belt. To Theresa it looked like a minicomputer. But to her surprise, Arginot spoke into it. She took advantage of the distraction to chase down one of her charges who was crawling across the kitchen floor toward the bedrooms.

"Yes, sir," she heard Arginot say. "We were just going over those details now. That'd be great. . . . Let me just check with Mrs. Hammond. . . ."

Arginot put his hand over the little device. "Reverend Hester would love to have you as his guest at his crusade Saturday night. We would put you up in New York City at our expense."

"Um . . . I don't know. I guess so," Theresa said, carrying the little boy back into the living room, where she squeaked a few toys to get his attention.

"Great." Arginot turned back to the phone. "She's in. Oh yeah, that would be great. How long do you need it to be?" He whispered to Theresa, "A short testimony in church." Then back into the phone, "I'll let her know." He paused and listened while Theresa fretted about the testimony. "I'll be going out to the square with Thomas tonight. You can let the show's producer know that this thing is far from over."

Though she was almost too nervous and intimidated to speak, Theresa knew she had to say something. She didn't want to appear ungrateful—but a testimony? And Thomas going back to the square?

"I'm not very good at testimonies," she confessed as Arginot hung up and clipped the device back on his belt. "And I really don't want Thomas going back out to the square with his manger scene. I'm dead set against that."

Arginot reached over and patted her hand. "Don't worry about the testimony," he cooed. "We have professionals that will help you put it together and memorize it. You'll just look over the heads of the audience and pretend there's nobody there. Our best testimonies come from folks just like you who are scared to death. God works best in our weaknesses."

Theresa knew that last part was true, but it still wasn't helping her roiling stomach.

"As for Thomas's going back out to the square, you've got

to trust our judgment on that, Theresa. Technically, Thomas will be my client, not you. Therefore, I've got to give *him* my best legal advice and let *him* make that decision. I'm just saying that if he does go out there, I'll go with him. And even if he doesn't, we're appealing his sentence to the Fourth Circuit Court of Appeals, so this thing isn't over." Arginot leaned forward a little and looked very sincere. "Do you believe God sent me here to help you?"

Though Theresa was having some doubts, she thought about the timing of his visit. He had knocked on the door in the middle of her chaotic prayer! How much more plain could God make it? Did she believe God sent him? "Yes."

"Then you've got to trust that He will help me make the right calls for you and Thomas."

It still didn't feel right. Things were happening way too fast. But Mr. Arginot was right in pointing out that Thomas had to make this call. Theresa knew her husband—nobody told him what to do.

"Will you at least try to talk Thomas out of going to the square?" she asked.

"I'll give him my best legal advice," Arginot replied. "I'll tell him we can appeal without violating the court order again. But, Theresa, if he insists on going to the square, I'll be there with him."

Something about the way he said all this left her unsettled. But she wrote it off to her own insecurities. What more could she ask him to do? "Okay," she said, reminding herself again that he had arrived during prayer.

"Good. Now you've got some packing to do for you and the kids. And keep in mind, it's cold in New York this time of year."

23

To get to Possum High on Friday night for Ajori's game, Jasmine had to drive down Main Street, right past the Possum town square. The varsity girls' game started at seven, and as usual, Jasmine was running a few minutes late. She felt the frustration rise when she saw the line of red taillights in front of her—bumper-to-bumper about two blocks from the square. A traffic jam in Possum? She'd never heard of such a thing.

Traffic came to a dead stop about a block from the square, so several drivers pulled their cars next to the curb and started walking. Pedestrians were streaming down the sidewalks dressed in heavy overcoats and wool hats, heading to the square. She noticed the temperature on the sign in front of the town bank. Forty-two degrees.

After five minutes that seemed like fifty-five, traffic started crawling again. As she approached the square on her right, she could see the floodlights. Television trucks jammed around the square had reduced the Main Street traffic to one lane—the opposite lanes taking turns under the direction of one of Possum's finest. Jasmine had never seen this many people congregate in one place in Possum, not even during her senior basketball season. There were families and senior citizens, teens and children. When Jasmine rolled down her passenger-side window, she could hear the Christmas carols being played by a band.

A band! It would have to be the high school marching band, which probably hadn't played a tune since the football season. There were vendors selling coffee and hot chocolate and even sweatshirts. The sweatshirt vendor had a sample raised high on a pole above his table for everyone to see. He was charging twenty bucks for a "No Room in the Square?" sweatshirt, and his line stretched for half a block.

Jasmine craned her neck to see if the main attraction for the night had staked out his turf. She yelled at a passerby on the sidewalk. "Is he out there?"

A teenager shrugged her shoulders. "We heard he was coming out around eight or so," she said. "But we wanted to get a good spot."

Though Jasmine had been wrestling with the issue all day, she still hadn't decided whether or not to withdraw from representing Thomas. All this excitement was making her think twice about backing out of the case. But what defense did he have? Especially if he were dumb enough to flaunt Ichabod's order one more time and set up his manger scene tonight.

Resisting the urge to pull over and join the crowd, Jasmine continued toward her alma mater. She had a sister to support. And based on what she had just seen, Ajori and her teammates could probably use every fan they could get.

By the time Jasmine arrived at the gym and joined her mom in the bleachers, Possum was already down by eight. There were so few spectators that the gym seemed deathly quiet—you could hear the squeak of shoes as the players made their cuts.

"Where're the cheerleaders?" Jasmine asked.

"Probably at the town square with everyone else," her mom said.

Franklin High hit a three. "Wish I could be at the square," one of the other moms said. Jasmine's mom shot her a look that could melt steel. "But then I'd miss the exciting comeback we're gonna make," the woman added.

Barker was prowling the sidelines, burying his head in his hands. "Patience, ladies, patience!" he'd scream whenever the Possum girls would dare to shoot. "Work it around for a better shot!"

Ajori clanged a three-pointer off the back rim. "You call that patience?" Barker yelled.

"Keep firing! They'll fall!" Jasmine's mom yelled.

"Is she wearing her hair different?" one of the ladies asked.

"Hands up!" another screamed.

Jasmine just shook her head. They were still in the first quarter, and Possum was now down twelve.

By the second quarter, Barker had turned his ire from his impatient team to the referees. He began complaining about every call, drawing his first technical for a childish display of foot stomping and pouting. A few minutes later Rebecca Arlington had to restrain him or he would have drawn his second.

"You tell 'em, Coach!" yelled Jasmine's mom, always the instigator. Barker turned and shot her a look.

The game's that way, Jasmine wanted to say, pointing at the court. Instead, she bit her tongue.

But Barker did not bite his. A few minutes before half-time, Barker detonated again. It happened at the end of a Franklin High fast break, after their star player, a girl nick-named Train, came barreling down the lane and mowed down Tamarika, who had established herself in perfect position to draw the charge.

Tamarika collected herself from the floor, checking to make sure all her parts were still intact, while the ref blew his whistle. "Blocking foul—" he motioned—"on number four." And Barker went into orbit.

He jumped from the bench and started screaming at the ref. "You're pathetic—you know that?" Then came a stream of curse words. "You're a disgrace to the game."

The ref tried to calm things down, first seeming to ignore Barker, then motioning for him to sit back down. Rebecca Arlington, the petite blonde assistant who treated ball games like a modeling opportunity, tried to do her part. She stood and put a hand on Barker's elbow. "Let it go, Coach." But in her heels and knee-length skirt, she was no match for Barker.

He shrugged her off and charged the ref like a bull.

Before Jasmine could blink, Barker was nose-to-nose with the startled ref. Bobby Knight would've been proud. Barker made a few more nasty comments in a tone so menacing and low that Jasmine couldn't hear what he said.

But the ref did. And it surprised no one when he slapped a second technical on Barker and pointed to the locker room door. Barker made one more comment; the ref's face registered one last look of surprise; then Barker stalked off the court.

Most eyes followed Barker, but Jasmine watched Rebecca. Jasmine's former classmate, whiter than normal, gathered the team around while the Franklin player took her foul shots. Rebecca seemed at a total loss for words but eventually mumbled something, and the players nodded. When play resumed, Rebecca returned to her seat on the bench, still faithfully keeping stats like an assistant coach, while her players charged around the floor, playing out of control like bumper cars at a theme park.

By halftime Franklin's lead had swelled to twenty-two.

The Possum players slumped toward their locker room, but Rebecca looked too petrified to follow them. First, she checked the book at the scorer's table; then she straightened up a few water bottles next to the bench, and finally, when she could apparently think of no other stalling tactics, she looked at Jasmine.

Rebecca shrugged her shoulders and held up her palms. *I'm clueless.* Jasmine stood and walked down the bleachers to the gym floor.

"What do I tell them?" Rebecca asked.

Jasmine bent down a little—even in heels, Rebecca wasn't five-eight—and explained a couple of adjustments that made Rebecca's eyes cloud over.

"Jasmine, you come tell them. They'll listen to you."

Jasmine protested but knew that Rebecca had a point. Jasmine allowed herself to hold out for half a minute before agreeing to accompany Rebecca into the locker room. "But I'm not staying if Barker's in there," she said.

"He won't be there," Rebecca responded. Before Jasmine could ask how Rebecca knew, she found herself following the assistant coach off the floor.

When Jasmine entered the locker room, she saw nothing but the tops of heads—a ponytail here, a headband there, a scrunchie holding a pile of hair in place. Most of the girls sat with their elbows on their thighs, staring at the floor, ready to absorb another well-earned verbal bashing. Jasmine glanced around the silent room—there was no sign of Barker.

"I've asked Jasmine to come in and talk to us," Rebecca said as heads sheepishly glanced up. "She says there're a few adjustments we need to make."

24

FROM THE LOCKER room to the bench was a natural transition. Sure, Rebecca was still the fill-in head coach, now sitting in the head coach's seat at the end of the bench— but Jasmine did all the yelling. Plus Jasmine had a brilliant strategy. She noticed that the other team's big girl was afraid to shoot from the outside. So Jasmine stuck her six-footer— Ginger—in the lane at the defensive end and told her not to worry about guarding anybody in particular. "Your only job," Jasmine told her, clenching her teeth so Ginger could feel the intensity, "is to be a lean, mean shot-blocking machine. That's your paint! Got it? *Your* paint! Anybody comes in there, you make 'em pay. Got it?"

"Yes, ma'am."

Ma'am? I'm only twenty-four, Jasmine wanted to say. But there was no time for that.

In the first three minutes, her strategy helped Franklin increase the lead from twenty-two to twenty-eight.

She subbed for Ginger and made the gangly senior sit next to her on the bench. "I thought I told you to block shots," Jasmine said.

"Sorry, Coach. I tried."

"Don't apologize."

"My bad." Ginger squirted some water in her mouth and started putting on her warm-up jacket.

"Take that off," Jasmine snapped. "You're going right back in." Ginger looked disappointed at the news.

"You like Coach Barker?" Jasmine asked.

"He's okay," Ginger said tentatively. "A little tough sometimes."

Ajori missed a jumper, and the Franklin girls were off and running to the other end. *No wonder Barker's always in a foul mood.*

"Barker ever call you any names?" Jasmine asked.

Silence.

"Did he?"

"He called me an uncoordinated geek once."

"Anything else?"

"A waste of six feet."

"What else?"

More hesitation. "He called me soft. He called me a little old lady. He called me stupid. He called me—"

"Enough." Jasmine put an arm around Ginger's shoulders and pointed to the court. "See those Franklin girls?" Ginger nodded. "Every one of 'em is Coach Barker. When they come into the lane, punish 'em for all those names they called you."

"Yes, ma'am."

"Go in for Tamarika."

At the next dead ball, Ginger went lumbering into the game and the fiery little point guard came out huffing and puffing. "They're fouling me every play, Coach." Tamarika plopped down next to Jasmine. "You need to get on the refs."

"Barker already tried that," Jasmine said matter-of-factly. While Tamarika fidgeted in her seat, Ginger flattened some poor Franklin girl who dared take the ball into Ginger's paint. She started helping the Franklin player up while looking at her coach for approval.

Jasmine motioned Ginger over to the bench while the Franklin girl took her foul shot.

"Nice foul," Jasmine said.

"Thanks."

"But what are you doing helping her up?"

"Huh?"

"Barker ever help you up?" Jasmine asked.

"No."

"Next time step over her and don't help her up. You only get five fouls; make 'em count."

Ginger reached up to tighten her scrunchie. "Sorry," she said. Jasmine gave her an evil eye. "I mean, forget you," Ginger said.

"Attagirl." Jasmine slapped her on the butt and returned to Tamarika.

"Barker never sits me out this long," the point guard complained.

"He must not realize how slow you are."

Tamarika furrowed her brow. "Whatchu talkin' 'bout, Coach?"

Jasmine just shrugged. "I don't know who you think you're fooling, but you're slower than half the white girls out there. Plus you play ball like a white girl—all deliberate and fundamental like some farm girl from Indiana. I thought you had jets."

Tamarika scowled. "You want speed?"

"Yeah. I want speed and I want hip-hop."

Tamarika's lips curled a little at the corners. "You want hip-hop?"

"And street ball—total trash-talking, hip-hopping, not-in-my-house, smashmouth street ball."

Now Tamarika smiled broadly, displaying big white teeth. "You sure, Coach?"

"I'm sure."

"It's hard to do that from the bench," Tamarika said.

"I know. Check in for Ajori."

Ajori came off the floor and headed for the end of the bench. Jasmine walked down and sat next to her.

"I think I had twenty-seven against Franklin my senior year," Jasmine said.

"So."

"You've only got six so far."

Ajori just watched the floor.

"'Course, I shot about fifteen threes," Jasmine said.

"Coach doesn't like the three-ball. Likes to pound it inside."

Jasmine made a show of surveying the gymnasium, then turned back to Ajori. "I don't see Coach in here."

About that time Tamarika made a beautiful move to the hoop, culminated by a slick no-look pass to Ginger. The pass surprised everyone, most of all Ginger. The ball bounced off her hands and out-of-bounds.

"Dad liked the three-ball," Jasmine said. "Said the high school game was a three-point game. Guess he didn't know what he was talking about."

Ajori snorted. "Don't try that Dr. Phil psychobull on me. Who made you coach, anyway?"

"Fine," Jasmine said, and she headed to the other end of the bench.

Two minutes later she heard a familiar voice behind her. "Put Ajori in!"

Jasmine turned and stared at her mom, who in turn nodded toward Ajori's end of the bench. *I thought you didn't yell at coaches,* Jasmine wanted to say. Instead, she shuffled down and sat next to Ajori.

"You ready?" Jasmine asked.

"Guess so."

Jasmine leaned toward her sister. "Look, I know you're having a tough game, a tough season. But this is your chance, Ajori. Coach isn't here. That excuse is gone. Show these fans what you can do if you're freed up to play."

Jasmine moved her legs back as Tamarika came skidding toward the bench, face-first, diving after a loose ball. She hopped up and looked at Jasmine. "Get my wingman back in here," she demanded, nodding toward Ajori. "We're comin' back, Coach." The lead had been whittled down to twenty-two.

Jasmine met Ajori's eyes. "How many threes you want?" Ajori asked.

"One per minute."

"Okay, *Coach*."

As Ajori jogged to the scorer's table, Jasmine thought about how weird it felt to be called coach by her little sister. *Coach* was a title reserved for some pretty special people. Her dad. Her college coach. Who in her life had been more important than them?

Ajori's first three was an air ball, but Jasmine didn't care. By the fourth quarter her kid sister had found her range. And Tamarika was making some of the wildest, funkiest passes the Possum gym had seen in a long time. Too bad nobody could catch them.

When Ginger fouled out on a clean block swatting some girl's shot back toward half-court, the few hardy fans remaining actually stood and cheered. And Jasmine nearly fainted when Ginger stared the ref down before heading to the bench.

"Attagirl," Jasmine said.

They lost by only twelve. And when Jasmine went into the locker room after the game, not a single head was hanging.

25

SATURDAY MORNING, DECEMBER 16

To Theresa it felt like ninety-eight degrees on the set of the *Morning Show*. She smiled nervously as a blonde-haired lady named Deborah introduced Theresa and her kids to the nation. Theresa felt like an idiot. They had insisted that she wear bright red lipstick and gobs of makeup. At least Thomas wouldn't be watching.

Tiger and Hannah were both sitting quietly with their hands in their laps. She noticed with embarrassment how fast they were growing. Tiger's pants were halfway up his shins, nearly showing off the tops of his cowboy boots. His skinny arms were keeping pace with his legs, and his suit-coat sleeves were also halfway up to his elbows. He and Hannah gawked openmouthed back and forth between the cameras and their host.

The only person who looked at ease, other than the host, was the Reverend Freddie Hester. The man had more makeup caked on than Theresa, though he passed on the lipstick. His hair stood up about four inches, then swept back over his head like the mane of a stallion. He was smiling as he looked straight into the camera as if he might kiss it at any moment.

"This was the scene at the Possum town square last night," Deborah said. In the monitors in front of them, Theresa could see her husband setting up his manger scene to the wild applause of half the town of Possum and a few hundred other onlookers. Tiger nudged Hannah, pointing at the camera. "Shh," Hannah said, though Tiger hadn't actually spoken.

"This morning, Thomas Hammond has been ordered to appear in court again to face further contempt charges."

Suddenly Deborah turned to face Theresa, concern etched deeply on the host's pretty face. "Are you worried about your husband having to spend more time in jail, perhaps even Christmas?"

Theresa's mouth was dry and her tongue unwieldy. "Um . . . yes, we're very worried."

"There are a lot of people who say your husband is well-intentioned but that he's going about this the wrong way. Even some respected church leaders believe that he shouldn't be defying a federal judge and the law. What would you say to them?"

Wow. Theresa didn't have the foggiest idea. In part, she agreed with these critics—but how could she say that? Before the show, Deborah had mentioned that she would ask a few easy questions about how this controversy made Theresa feel. Deborah said she wanted to put a personal face on the matter. But Deborah had never mentioned these accusations by respected church leaders.

"I guess that's their opinion," Theresa managed. She was immediately struck by how dumb that sounded. Of course it was their opinion; hadn't the host already established that?

"But do you agree with it?"

Reverend Hester chuckled, and the cameras swung toward him. "Obviously she doesn't agree with it," he said boldly. "That's why this family—" he made a sweeping gesture toward Theresa and the kids—"is taking this courageous stand. The worship of God trumps the laws of men. That's a principle as old as the ancient Jewish prophet Daniel."

For the next minute or so, the reverend lectured the host on the story of Daniel and the lions' den while Deborah desperately tried to interrupt. Only the kids seemed the least bit interested. When Hester finished, Deborah turned a little more in her chair so she was looking right at Theresa, literally giving the reverend the cold shoulder.

"What would you say to a Muslim who wanted to erect a memorial to Muhammad on the Possum town square during the holiday season?"

Theresa didn't know. Suddenly she felt like she was the one on trial, not her husband. "I guess I'd tell him that in America he should be free to do it. But I don't know why he'd want to—since Christmas is a *Christian* holiday."

Deborah shifted forward a little in her seat. "But wouldn't you agree that a manger scene in the town square can be potentially divisive? Some would say that at Christmas, of all times, we ought to put aside our differences and strive for peace. Why is your husband so insistent on pushing this now?"

Theresa looked down for a moment and thought about this. "For Thomas it's a matter of principle."

"And an important one at that," the reverend said. But Deborah cut him off before he could get rolling.

"We're almost out of time. Let's quickly hear from the Hammond children," she said. "Hannah, what do you think about what your daddy is doing?"

"He's very brave," Hannah said, staring wide-eyed into the camera.

This brought a big smile from Hester.

"Have you seen the Christmas tree in Rockefeller Plaza yet?" Deborah asked.

Hannah scrunched her face in confusion.

"Not yet," Hester said. "But we're going to see it this afternoon, just before our Christmas Crusade in Madison Square Garden."

Deborah turned toward Tiger. "Now, for Tiger—" she glanced at the televangelist—"and only for Tiger—what do you think of your daddy?"

"He's brave," Tiger said quickly, parroting Hannah. "And strong."

Theresa smiled to herself. Tiger always liked to one-up his sister.

Deborah smiled too. "And what have you asked Santa to bring you for Christmas?"

Tiger froze. Theresa could almost see the wheels turning in her son's mind. She wondered if she should interrupt and tell the host they didn't believe in Santa. But as usual, she was a few seconds too slow.

"A puppy," Tiger said.

At this, Hannah's mouth opened into a perfect little circle and she put her hand over it as if Tiger had just cussed on national television.

"And what about your daddy—did you ask Santa for anything about your daddy?"

"That he won't be in jail."

"Awww," said one of the women operating a camera.

"And there you have it," Deborah said, looking into the camera. "A judge determined to follow the law and a father determined to follow his conscience. This morning, we've talked with the family members stuck in the middle."

26

ON SATURDAY MORNING Jasmine's mom, as usual, was the first one up. By the time Jasmine made it to the kitchen, the coffee was brewed, the pancakes were piled high on a plate, and the bacon was frying.

"Your client made the front page." Bernice handed the paper to Jasmine.

"Manger Madness Escalates" proclaimed the headline of the *Virginian-Pilot*. Jasmine skimmed the article quickly—all the predictable stuff about the separation of church and state and the rule of law. Halfway through the first column was a quote from David A. Arginot III, identified as the new attorney for Thomas Hammond, predicting all manner of victory in the courts.

"He's not my client, Mom. I withdrew." Jasmine set the paper down and poured a cup of coffee.

"Thought you had twenty-four hours to change your mind," her mom said.

"I did. But Thomas wouldn't return my calls last night. And now the paper says he's got a new lawyer." Jasmine wasn't quite sure how she felt about all this. Relieved? Yes. Now her New York job was intact. But also disappointed. "Besides, he wouldn't follow my advice."

"His loss," her mom said.

They turned on the television while Jasmine sipped her coffee and helped herself to a couple of pancakes. Three times during breakfast, Bernice went upstairs to rouse Ajori. Finally, at just a few minutes before nine, Ajori stumbled into the kitchen, earphones and iPod already in place. She was dressed in her workout clothes and sandals.

"You might want to heat up those pancakes," Bernice said.

"I'll eat later."

"You want to call him again this morning?" Jasmine asked.

"Huh?" Ajori took out an earbud.

"You want to call him again this morning?"

Ajori snorted. "Are you kidding?"

A few minutes later, Ajori and Jasmine put on their fleeces, grabbed their gym bags, and headed out the door.

They waited at the gym, along with the rest of the Possum Lady Bulldogs, for nearly forty-five minutes. The whole thing had been Jasmine's idea. After last night's game, she spent nearly an hour talking to the team about Coach Barker. "He got thrown out tonight sticking up for you," Jasmine explained. "I don't like his style either, but he's just trying to make you the best ballplayers possible."

The girls were a tough sell—in part because Jasmine didn't believe it herself. But she knew it was the right thing to tell them.

She also knew that after every Friday night loss, Barker would call for a brutal Saturday morning practice. Though it took every one of her legally trained arguing muscles, Jasmine talked the girls into calling Barker and letting him know that they would be at the gym Saturday morning. Ajori had left the message on behalf of the team.

But now, forty-five minutes after the scheduled starting time, Barker still hadn't shown. "You want to call him again?" Jasmine asked her little sister.

"Uh . . . no?" her sister declared as sarcastically as possible.

As the team disbanded and the vehicles left the parking lot, Jasmine thought about Barker and grew furious. What kind of coach quit on his team? left his players hanging? What could he possibly be thinking?

On the drive home, with Ajori riding in the passenger seat in her iPod-induced haze, Jasmine thought about the terrible chemistry between Barker and his team. This, in turn, made her miss her dad so much that she had to fight back the tears. Barker liked a style straight from the fifties. Her dad understood players. Her dad knew the game. He loved his teams. Her dad would never quit on his kids, even if they didn't run the offense very well.

Quitting. A sudden pang of guilt tingled through Jasmine's spine. Wasn't that her dad's number one principle? *Never ever quit. Quitters never win; winners never quit. When the going gets tough, the tough get going. Can't never could.* The clichés that Jasmine hated so much now stormed through her brain.

Whatever it takes . . . and a little bit more. The quote her dad gave the paper after the state championship loss: *"This team's never lost a game, though the clock ran out on us a few times."* The sign over the locker room door as they entered the gym: "Sacrifice Self for Team."

What would he think of her now? Bailing on Thomas. Running from a legal fight just because her client wouldn't follow her advice . . . just because a future employer didn't want the publicity.

She knew the answer as soon as she allowed herself to ask the question. But there was nothing she could do about it now except to pray for one more chance.

27

With each talk show on Saturday morning, Theresa's doubts increased. Every host had questions that she couldn't answer. What about the Muslims? Couldn't Thomas set up the manger scene on church property? And the toughest one: Did she agree that the manger scene was just part of the history of a secular national holiday that was no longer regarded as a religious event?

Of course she didn't agree, but she didn't want to disrespect the town's justification for displaying the manger scene, either. Instead, she stumbled around and looked like a fool. Eventually, she settled for her old standby: "That was their opinion."

After the shows, a young assistant for Reverend Hester

named Johnny whisked them around New York City. It was overwhelming—all the people and the monstrous buildings—and Theresa couldn't help but stare at the tops of the huge skyscrapers like the tourist she was. The wind whipped through the streets and cut right through her wool winter coat. She hoped to see snow, but Johnny told her it was too cold to snow. Instead, their little crew stepped around the slush left from an earlier snowfall, with little piles of black snow and ice lining parts of the curb.

They spent a few minutes gawking at the giant tree at Rockefeller Center and watching the ice skaters. "They're not very good," Tiger commented. Then Johnny hailed a cab, and they took a breathtaking ride to Herald Square and pushed their way through the revolving doors into Macy's department store. It was the biggest store Theresa had ever seen—you could probably fit Possum inside it twice—and it was absolutely jammed with people from pretty much every country on earth. Before long they were swept up the escalators with the mobs headed for the toy department. When they got there, Tiger and Hannah wandered around for a half hour with their mouths agape, expanding their Christmas lists while exploring endless rows of gadgets and toys. Their trips to the Dollar Store would never be the same again.

Just before they left, Theresa noticed Hannah linger near a shelf filled with dolls and become rather quiet. The dolls were chubby little replicas of babies that reminded Theresa of Bebo.

She ran her hand down Hannah's hair. "You okay?"

"I wish Daddy could be here."

"Me too. But Daddy's got a good lawyer. He'll be fine." Theresa had explained to the kids that Thomas had to be in court this morning. Even in the midst of touring New York City, she thought of little else.

"When will we know what the judge said?" Hannah asked.

"Daddy's lawyer is going to call Mr. Johnny as soon as court's over." She knelt down and gave Hannah a reassuring hug. The little girl worried enough for both of them.

"Will he go to jail?" It was the third time she had asked that question.

Theresa leaned back, still kneeling, and looked into Hannah's troubled eyes. She gently brushed the hair out of her daughter's face. "Hannah, you know I can't say for sure. But God won't let anything bad happen."

"Look out!" Tiger yelled. Nearly thirty feet away, he had discovered a small battery-powered replica of a motorcycle and climbed on board. The thing was low to the ground, and now he was cruising down the aisle, dodging legs, and heading straight for Theresa. Johnny watched and smiled broadly.

"Mom! Look at this!" Tiger yelled . . . just before the crash.

★

They were heading back to the hotel when the call came on Johnny's cell phone. He answered and listened for a moment. "She's right here," he said before handing the phone to Theresa.

"Mrs. Hammond, this is David Arginot. Are you enjoying your time in New York?"

"It's been great." Theresa waited, not interested in small talk.

"Well," Arginot said, "there's no easy way to say this. Thomas is back in jail. We had a tough morning . . . but we'll get this reversed on appeal, I can promise you that. . . ."

Theresa felt like she'd been body slammed. Jail again! Despite her fervent prayers! Arginot rattled on about the details of the hearing—words that didn't penetrate Theresa's stupor. She tried to act strong in front of the kids, gritting her teeth and forcing back the tears. She didn't want to speak for fear the dam would break, but there was something she *had* to know—right now.

"How long?" she asked, interrupting an explanation of the appeals process.

"Excuse me?"

"How long is he in for?" She glanced at the kids. Tiger stared at her. Hannah had her eyes closed in prayer.

"Until he agrees not to set up the manger scene again on the Possum town square, or at midnight following Christmas Day, whichever comes first."

"Lord, help us."

28

A PHONE CALL with Thomas that afternoon eased Theresa's mind somewhat. Still, it was hard to enjoy the plush New York hotel room knowing that Thomas would be spending another night in the cold confines of a Norfolk federal holding cell.

"Can't you just promise that you won't do it again?" Theresa asked. "You've already made your point."

Thomas breathed into the phone, and Theresa immediately felt guilty for pressuring him. "You know I can't do that, Theresa. You've just got to be strong."

Theresa was tired of being strong, though she didn't say that to Thomas.

A few hours later, as she stepped into the greenroom

backstage at Madison Square Garden, Theresa had to summon every ounce of courage and strength that she had left. For nearly an hour the folks working for the Christmas Crusade told Theresa to relax and then did everything possible to make her nervous. First, they whisked her kids off to some "Bible Land" program that would take place in a side auditorium while the adults met on the main floor of the Garden. Then came the heavy makeup and the instructions about where she would be sitting onstage and how she should not worry about the large crowd but just consider them all part of her family. "It's like having a nice little chat with a few thousand of your closest friends," they joked. Then they practiced the questions that the Reverend Hester might ask her, listened to her answers, and gave her some gentle pointers about how to phrase things a little differently.

"It's okay to cry," one of the ladies told her.

"Yeah, I'd be surprised if you didn't cry," another said, "considering what your husband's going through."

Theresa got the message, though she had no plans to deliver on manufactured tears.

Ten minutes before showtime, the three handlers who had been tending to Theresa pronounced her ready, because they had bigger fish to fry. The Reverend Freddie Hester had arrived in an uproar, shouting out instructions while they slapped on his makeup.

"Where's the video for the Gateway Christmas Children's Project?" he barked. Assistants scurried, and a few seconds later it was playing on a television in the greenroom. It was, Theresa thought, a touching story about the need to support some orphanages in Kenya.

"Will that work?" Johnny asked anxiously as soon as the tape had finished.

"Two minutes!" someone called out.

"Guess it will have to," the reverend said.

Everyone huddled and held hands. The reverend prayed while some handlers adjusted his mike and earpiece.

"Glory!" he shouted and headed onstage.

Theresa watched the first part of the service on the monitor in the greenroom. She was nearly sick with fright, wringing her hands and praying fervently for the strength to get through. She practiced her lines over and over in her head, determined not to mess up a single word. The singing was awesome, though she could hardly enjoy it in her frenzied state, and the Reverend Hester sure knew how to fire up the troops. As the Christmas Children's Project video played, cameras panned the audience, catching more than a few glistening eyes.

A few minutes before Theresa's scheduled appearance, the Reverend Hester called people forward for prayer. As was his custom, he wandered down among those gathering at the altar, sticking a mike in front of them and asking them to describe their various ailments. He had an uncanny ability to call many of them by name and miraculously list their disabilities even before they described them. Then he would pray over them with great furor, and they would be slain in the Spirit and drop on the ground, many times rising without a trace of their former problems.

"Mrs. Hammond, it's just about time. After this prayer time, there will be one song and then your interview."

Theresa wanted to know if she had time to throw up or at least hit the bathroom one last time, but they were already ushering her backstage. There was another area with a few chairs where they left Theresa, promising to return momentarily. She sat there patiently for a moment, but then noticed a bank of backstage monitors a little closer to the stage. Several men and women were stationed in front of them and wore earphones. They watched the monitors intently.

Curious, Theresa moved close enough so she could watch the monitors but also glance around occasionally at where her handlers had left her.

"That's Jamie," one of the men was saying, reading off a card. "She's got breast cancer."

On the monitors, Theresa saw the reverend approach a young woman and put his arm around her. "Jamie," he said, "do you believe the Lord can heal your cancer?"

The woman looked astonished, nodding and blurting, "Yes, yes, yes." The reverend prayed and Jamie hit the floor. This went on for a few more minutes, a minor uproar occurring backstage when the reverend got a name wrong.

"I said 'Misty,' not 'Missy,'" one of the men said to another backstage.

"You've got to enunciate more clearly," the other man shot back. "The reverend will not be happy."

"Just to your right," another person said, apparently speaking into the reverend's earpiece. Theresa felt guilty for listening to all this. "A young mother named Kelly has a two-year-old baby with a blood disorder."

Lord! The mother of a two-year-old! Theresa felt the air leave her lungs. A year and a half ago, her own Joshie had died from appendicitis just months short of his second birthday. Thomas and Theresa prayed for three days, believing in a miracle, before they sought medical help. Theresa would never forgive herself.

She wanted to rush into the sanctuary and tell this woman to get help! *Pray hard but trust the doctors that God gives us as well!* Instead, the woman was affirming her faith that God was healing her son while the reverend prayed for a miracle that would be a sign for the watching world.

Theresa felt a gentle hand on her arm and turned. "It's time, Mrs. Hammond," one of the backstage assistants said.

Theresa shuffled nervously onstage and performed her lines nearly flawlessly, though her eyes stayed bone dry throughout. The reverend gushed about how proud he was to be able to assist the courageous Hammond family. He bragged on the legal prowess of attorney David Arginot III and displayed a toll-free number on the big screen for donations to the cause. In addition, the reverend said, they would be taking up a special Christmas offering in just a few minutes, with every dime going to the Thomas Hammond Legal Defense Fund to protect Christmas in America.

When the reverend finished, Theresa walked offstage to the thunderous applause of a grateful audience. She located Johnny and insisted that he help her find her kids. Though Johnny tried to talk her out of it, Theresa also insisted that she and the kids take a cab back to the hotel. She kept saying that she just needed some time alone, but in truth she didn't want to be around the ministry staff for even one more hour.

That night, after the kids were asleep, Theresa spent a long time staring at the ceiling and thinking about Kelly and her two-year-old child. She prayed for this woman she hardly knew, bonded by the shared heartache of seeing their children suffer. She also made up her mind that when she visited

Thomas on Sunday, she would tell him everything that had happened at Madison Square Garden. She knew Thomas, and she knew he wouldn't want the help of a group that used earpieces and cue cards to perform pretend miracles of healing. She wondered where they got that information on the cards, but she also realized it didn't really matter. If Thomas agreed, they would call Jasmine and beg her to come back on the case. After all, Jasmine couldn't do any worse than Mr. Arginot had done. And Jasmine understood the people of Possum—people like Thomas and Theresa.

Theresa didn't want to be a national celebrity, helping raise money for the Reverend Hester's television ministry. She just wanted Thomas out of jail. She just wanted things to be normal again.

And more than anything else, she wanted the one thing she knew she could never have: Joshie. She just wanted to hold him one more time.

29

Monday, December 18

Jasmine hated it when she did this. Her first morning to sleep in—no exams, no school pressures, no Hammond case hanging over her head—and she woke up at 7:30 and couldn't go back to sleep. She planned on staying in Possum with her mom and Ajori through Christmas; then she would return to her apartment in Virginia Beach.

She listened to Ajori stumble around a little as she got ready for school, her hair dryer and CD player from the bedroom next door erasing any hope of Jasmine's going back to sleep. She grabbed the covers and rolled over angrily, burying her ears in the pillow. Little sisters were such a pain!

After Ajori left, Jasmine headed downstairs.

"Good morning, baby," Jasmine's mom said, kissing her on the forehead.

"Coffee," Jasmine groaned. A few minutes later they were discussing shopping plans for the day. Jasmine's Christmas shopping so far had been limited to law school friends—she had zero gifts for family members. But shopping was her mom's specialty, and they eagerly made plans to attack the Tidewater malls until they had blisters on their feet.

"Hang on a second," Jasmine said, catching a mention of the manger case on the *Today* show. "I want to hear this."

David Arginot looked dapper in a three-button suit and light blue power tie, live from the studios in New York. He crossed his legs and gazed directly into the camera, explaining that he would be filing an appeal later in the day that would undoubtedly be successful. He leveled some thinly veiled criticisms of Judge Cynthia Baker-Kline and bemoaned the fact that a good man like Thomas Hammond was in jail. His host had some skeptical questions, but David handled them all with a bright smile and genuine charm. The man was a pro.

"Looks like Thomas is in good hands," Jasmine said. She had tried to call the Hammond house the prior day but got only their answering machine. She still found it hard to believe that Theresa and Thomas didn't have a cell phone. How did they live like that?

"Then why's he sitting in jail while his lawyer gets famous on TV?" Bernice asked.

"He's just doing his job," Jasmine responded, though she didn't believe it either. "Part of representing a client these days is winning the PR battle."

Her mom grabbed the remote and changed the channel.

Another talk show was promising its own interview with Arginot later that morning. Suddenly her mom had an urge to check ESPN. "Did ODU play last night?" she asked, though Jasmine was pretty sure that her mom already knew the answer.

Theresa couldn't watch television without running into an interview with David A. Arginot III. He apparently did nothing but float from one television studio to another, repeating his mantra about what a great American family the Hammonds were and how they were certain to win on appeal. Other commentators painted a bleaker picture of Mr. Arginot's chances with the Fourth Circuit. Meanwhile, Thomas sat in jail, and the Reverend Hester collected checks. The whole thing upset Theresa so much that she turned off the television and vowed not to watch it again until the case was over.

She wondered if Jasmine was up yet—it was only 8:30. Last night Thomas had agreed to fire Arginot if Jasmine would take the case. And if she wouldn't? "Then God's telling us to stay with Arginot," Thomas said. Theresa wasn't so sure.

She started to dial and then decided to give it a few more minutes. She would call Jasmine at nine. Jasmine was a law student and most law students liked to sleep in. Though Theresa knew she was making excuses, she allowed herself to get away with it. She *hated* asking people for favors. *Thomas, why do you put me through this?*

Ten minutes before her self-imposed deadline, she heard a knock on the door. She walked slowly to the miniblinds and peeked out, expecting someone from the press. Instead, there was nobody on the stoop, though she did see a car pulling away from the trailer. Was it some kind of prank? People didn't knock and run unless they're doing something ugly. Before going outside to check around, she made sure Elizabeth and her buddies were in the living room and secured the child gates to keep them there.

Then she cracked open the door and looked down. She stared at a gray plastic crate with a door on one end that had miniature bars over it. It had a Christmas card on top with the names Hannah, John Paul, and Elizabeth on it, and Theresa knew it could mean only one thing.

She stooped and looked through the bars. "Awww," she said before she could catch herself. It was an itty-bitty cocker spaniel—white with light brown markings—all curled up and shivering in one corner of the crate. "You're so cute," Theresa said, thinking about Tiger's request on national television. *But how can I deal with a puppy right now?* Behind the crate, someone had also left a small bag of puppy food, a box of bone-shaped puppy treats, a water bowl and food bowl, a leash, a miniature orange squeaky basketball, and a rope with frayed ends.

She dragged the crate and accessories inside, putting them on the tile kitchen floor. When she opened the crate, the puppy looked out at Theresa with big, sad eyes under a furrowed brow, eyes made even more pitiful by its long, floppy ears. She felt her heart melt and gently picked up the puppy, noticed it was a he, and held him against her body. She felt the little guy quiver. Then she saw a manila envelope taped to the side of the crate.

She placed the puppy on the floor and opened the envelope. There were a number of papers, including a certificate of pedigree. A purebred! Theresa looked down at the little furball, who was already exploring, nose to the ground, floppy ears dragging along. Elizabeth had pulled herself up at the gate and was squealing with excitement.

The puppy's mom was named Brown Eyed Daisy; the dad, Oliver Wendell Holmes. There were four generations of cocker spaniels listed, all with fancy names and colors noted. There was also the name of a breeder on the certificate. Theresa decided to give him a call.

But first—the puppy was chewing on one of Tiger's old sneakers that her son had left by the front door! Theresa picked the puppy up again, resisting the urge to give him a name because she knew she wouldn't be able to give him up if she did. How could she possibly deal with a dog in the midst of all the other turmoil going on in her life? He would need shots, food, and house-training. And she had no idea how he might do with the toddlers she cared for all day long.

She carried the puppy over to Elizabeth. "Puppy," Theresa said. Elizabeth tried to repeat the word, but it sounded more like "puh-puh-puh." "Puppy," Theresa said again. She guided her daughter's hand to help her pet the puppy without grabbing its hair. Elizabeth's eyes lit up and she bounced up and down.

Theresa knew that if Tiger and Hannah saw the puppy, it would be over. This called for quick thinking and decisive action—neither of which she considered her strong points. She hugged him tight to her chest because he couldn't stop shaking, the puppy was so nervous. And then—yuck! A warm wetness drizzled down her arm. She rushed toward the trailer door with her newest problem child.

He had gone all over her! *The story of my life,* she thought. *You're not the first one with that idea, little fella.*

She set him down outside, and he scurried around the yard, sniffing and wagging his tail as if he had finally found his perfect family. And every time Theresa made a move toward him to pick him up again, he darted away. The game was on. It took her ten minutes and two puppy treats to get him back inside.

★

Jasmine tried to act nonchalant as Theresa detailed her problems over the phone. Theresa said she would understand if Jasmine couldn't do it. She knew how hard it could be to represent Thomas. After all, she was married to him. But Theresa and Thomas had talked it over—they *really* wanted Jasmine to handle their case instead of this fancy lawyer from Reverend Hester's organization.

Jasmine fully intended to say yes. She had thought long and hard about the way Coach Barker had deserted her sister's team. Her own dad's anti-quitting rhetoric had been ringing in her ears since last Saturday. Now she was being given a second chance. But she also knew how to take advantage of leverage. And she would never have more than she did right now.

"Will Thomas follow my advice?"

This brought silence. "Yes, I certainly hope so. But he's not willing to tell the judge that he won't go back out there."

"So we're back where we started."

More silence. "I guess so, Jasmine. I don't know what else to say."

The next request surprised Jasmine. "Can you hang on for a second?"

"Sure." Jasmine heard Theresa set down the phone, and she immediately started second-guessing herself. *Did I push too hard? say something that offended her?* It was a long couple of minutes before Theresa got back on the line.

"Sorry," Theresa said, "I had a little emergency." Much to Jasmine's relief, Theresa explained about her still-nameless puppy, the one who had just eaten half a sock and thrown up all over the kitchen floor.

This time Jasmine didn't try to play it coy. "I'm ready to represent Thomas," she said. "I think we can win this case on appeal, and I think we can get a decision before Christmas. But I'll need a supervising lawyer, and nobody knows the case as well as Arginot. Maybe we could ask him to stay on but let me be the lead lawyer."

This suggestion was met with silence.

"Or maybe not," Jasmine said. "But I thought it was at least worth suggesting."

"I'm sorry," Theresa responded. "I've got nothing against Mr. Arginot. It's just that Thomas and I don't want to be used as a fund-raising tool by Reverend Hester. We've got problems with some of his theology."

"I can understand that." Then Jasmine had a thought. "Would you be willing to let Arginot stay on if Hester couldn't use your case to raise money?"

"I guess so."

"Good. Then I'll immediately file a motion to get back in the case and note our appeal." Jasmine swallowed hard— she didn't like demoting people, even people as deserving of a demotion as Arginot. "I'll call Arginot so you don't have to."

There was a long pause, and it sounded like Theresa was sniffling. "I can't tell you how grateful we are," she said at last. "This whole thing has just been overwhelming."

"I can't even imagine," Jasmine replied. "But things will calm down in the next few days. They've got to."

"I sure hope you're right," Theresa said, though she didn't sound convinced.

30

JASMINE WAS A charter member of the Internet and IM generation, so she hated making phone calls. The rules of her generation were simple: Do everything online. IM is preferred; e-mail is old school. Cell phones are best used for text messaging and for talking to friends. Cell phone calls to a stranger are to be avoided at all costs and are almost as outdated as snail mail. Never, ever write a letter!

But this afternoon Jasmine was out of choices. She had two phone calls to make and neither would be any fun. She dialed the cell phone of David Arginot, hoping for voice mail. Instead, he answered.

After they exchanged pleasantries and Jasmine told him what a good job he was doing on television (a small lie that wouldn't really do much harm), she jumped right into the real reason for her call. "Thomas and Theresa have retained me again to serve as lead counsel for the rest of the case. I filed the paperwork with the court about an hour ago. Since I'm only a third-year law student and I need a supervising lawyer, they're asking you to stay on as well, though I'm the one who will take the lead in court." She paused and braced herself.

Arginot laughed out loud. "Let me get this straight. You want David Arginot to carry the bags of a third-year law student who's never tried a case?"

"What I want doesn't matter. But yes, that's what the client wants. And did I mention you'd have to do it for free? Reverend Hester will have to agree not to use this case for fund-raising purposes."

Arginot snorted. "Nothing personal, Jasmine, but that's not going to happen. Since you're just a law student, let me explain a few facts about the real world. Number one, David Arginot never works for free. Number two, you've got to file a motion asking the court to allow you back into the case—"

"Done."

"Congratulations. Number three, you've got to find someone to supervise you, because I'm sure not going to do it."

"I can find someone else if I need to."

"And number four, the judge has to allow this to happen, which I doubt she'll do. Even if she's willing, she won't do it without a hearing. And since I'm busy working on the appeal right now, I won't be available for a hearing until sometime later this week, and by then it will be too late."

Jasmine waited a few beats in order to calm down. Yes, he

was condescending. And yes, he was arrogant. But Jasmine needed someone to supervise her on this case, and Arginot was the only other lawyer up to speed right now.

"The judge thought you might say something like that," Jasmine replied. "So after she read my motion to rejoin the case, she called me and asked me to make this phone call at her secretary's desk, just outside the judge's chambers. She said if you objected, I should come inside her chambers, and we could call you back on the speakerphone so we can resolve this situation immediately."

Jasmine smiled at the judge's secretary as she heard Arginot inhale sharply. "You're at the judge's office?"

"Yes, sir."

"And she asked you to do it this way?"

"She did."

"Don't you see, Jasmine? She just wants you to handle the appeal so that she won't get overturned. She knows I'll get her reversed."

"Do you want me to get her on the speakerphone in her office so you can tell her that yourself?"

A big sigh. "No, that won't be necessary. You can take the lead in the courtroom, but you need to at least allow me to handle the press."

Jasmine considered this for an instant. It wasn't perfect, but then things seldom were. "At no cost."

"What's your client got against Hester?"

"*Our* client, Mr. Arginot. And that's beside the point. Are you willing to do this pro bono, or should I get somebody else?"

"All right," he said. "I don't like it, but it doesn't appear that I have much choice unless I'm willing to let you bumble through this case without me. And as we both know, the precedent at stake is too important for me to do that." Jasmine smiled to herself as she listened to this face-saving lecture. "Tell your client it's an early Christmas present," Arginot sputtered.

Jasmine thanked him and got off the phone as quickly as possible before Arginot could change his mind. Ichabod leaned against her door and smiled. "Nicely done," she said.

"Thank you, Your Honor."

"Now go do us all a favor and tell your client to learn a little respect for the rule of law. You can still appeal my decision even if he's not sitting in jail."

Jasmine didn't know what to say. She was grateful that Judge Baker-Kline had allowed her back on the case, but this was pushing a little too hard.

"I understand that, Your Honor. But Mr. Hammond has his reasons."

"So do I, Ms. Woodfaulk. So do I."

★

Jasmine made the second phone call she was dreading on the way to the law school library. This time, she talked to one secretary, one receptionist, one paralegal, and eventually ended up in Pearson Payne's voice mail. Ten minutes later he called back.

He was not happy to learn that she would be back in the case. "That French lawyer working for that televangelist is not doing you any favors," Pearson said. "He's filling up the airwaves with all kinds of bigoted nonsense. You wouldn't believe how many of my partners have said how grateful they are that you're off the case. What am I supposed to tell them now?"

How about telling them the truth? Jasmine wanted to say. But she found 115,000 reasons to swallow those words. "I don't know, Mr. Payne. I'm sorry, but I need to do this."

"Think about the future, Jazz. This case might seem big now, but it's nothing compared to the cases you'll be handling if you come to Gold, Franks."

Jasmine hesitated. She didn't want to argue with Pearson Payne. "It's not the size of the case, Mr. Payne—"

"Pearson."

"Right. Pearson. It's just that I feel strongly about this. It's something I really need to do."

Pearson let silence be his answer. After he had made his point, he spoke softly, accenting his disappointment. "I'll do what I can, Jazz. But I can't promise you that we won't revoke our offer. A lot of our clients see this differently than you. And my partners don't like our recruits to create problems with the clients."

"I know," Jasmine said. "I wish there were some other way."

When she hung up, she realized how much she liked Pearson Payne. He was the kind of lawyer she hoped to become. And the last thing in the world she wanted to do was upset him. Well, maybe the second-to-last thing. The last thing would be to bail on a deserving client.

Quitters never win. To be able to look at herself in the mirror, she *had* to do this, even if it cost her the best job she would ever be offered. How dumb was that? Sometimes she wished her dad had been anything but a basketball coach.

31

WHEN THERESA CALLED the breeder, the man acted like he worked for the CIA. "Your puppy is the runt of the litter," he told Theresa. Traditionally, the owner of the sire got to pick one puppy from the litter for himself or herself. That person had been very clear that he or she didn't want his or her name divulged to anybody who called with a question. According to the breeder, the owner of the sire swore him to secrecy, saying the puppy would be a special and mysterious Christmas gift for somebody.

"Are the dogs good with little kids?" Theresa asked.

"The best," the breeder said. "Especially if they're around children while the dogs are still puppies."

"How big will he get?" Theresa asked.

"Thirty pounds max—a great inside dog." The breeder went into a long spiel about how playful and even-tempered cocker spaniels are. "What did you name him?"

"I'm waiting till the older kids get home." When Theresa hung up the phone, she felt a little guilty for pretending she might keep him. And the puppy didn't make things any easier when he looked at her with those droopy little eyes and wagged his tail so hard that his entire backside shook.

★

The kids were pretty quiet as Theresa drove them home from school. She parked the minivan next to the trailer, and the kids got out without a word, helping her drag "the babies" out of their car seats and carry them inside.

"Let's put the babies in the living room and put up the gate," Theresa told Tiger and Hannah. "Then I want you guys to wait in the kitchen and cover your eyes."

A surprise! This perked the kids up a little. After taking care of the toddlers, they stood with their hands over their eyes, still wearing their winter coats, as Theresa went to the bedroom to get the puppy out of his crate. "No peeking," she called out.

She quietly placed the puppy on the kitchen floor. "You can look now," she said, thinking it was a miracle that Tiger had not already done so.

Hannah dropped her hands, spotted the cocker spaniel, then jumped and squealed in delight. She covered her mouth and stifled another scream. Tiger darted around her and cornered the puppy so the mauling could begin. The kids loved all over the hyper little guy while Theresa tried valiantly to explain that they couldn't keep him. The puppy got a little scared and tucked his tail between his legs as the kids passed him back and forth. He was looking at Theresa, practically begging her to bail him out. When he realized it wasn't going to happen, he resorted to Plan B. The kids dropped him on the floor immediately.

"He does that when he gets excited," Theresa said.

"Gross," Tiger said.

"He's so cute," Hannah said. "Can't we keep him, Momma? Pleeeeease!"

Within seconds, the begging started in earnest. They both promised to feed and water the puppy every day, take him for walks, train him in the most sophisticated tricks, and clean their rooms every day for the rest of their lives. Without hesitation, both offered to forgo any other Christmas gift if they could just keep the puppy. Hannah even offered to throw in next year's birthday as well, though Tiger was conspicuously silent on that point.

The kids were relentless, and everyone involved knew that it would be only a matter of minutes before Theresa would crack. Secretly, Theresa was on the side of the kids—how could she not be when she looked into those sad brown puppy eyes? She knew Thomas wouldn't approve. If they ever did get a dog, he'd want some kind of huge outdoor mutt that he could take into the woods logging with him, not some prissy indoor puppy. But as far as Theresa was concerned, Thomas had forfeited his vote by getting himself thrown into jail. If he wanted to veto the puppy, he needed to be home to do it.

"If we did keep him," Theresa said, "what would you name him?"

Because he came as a Christmas gift, Hannah suggested "Angel."

"Mom said he's a boy," Tiger responded. "Angel's a girl's name."

Hannah pondered this for a moment. "Then how 'bout Gabriel," she said, showing off her almost-encyclopedic biblical knowledge—it seemed the girl remembered everything she heard in Sunday school. "Gabriel is the name of an angel."

Tiger studied the puppy. "He doesn't look like a Gabriel."

Hannah grunted and threw her hands in the air. "Then you name him."

"What about Spot?" Tiger suggested. "He's got a light brown spot right in the middle of his forehead."

Hannah made a noise like this was the dumbest idea she had ever heard in her long and well-traveled little life. "Everybody names their dog Spot," she complained. "See Spot run." Then she had another idea. "What about King? There are kings in the Christmas story too."

Tiger looked skeptical but didn't reject the name outright. His face brightened. "His nickname could be King Kong."

So King it was, though Theresa didn't think this innocent little puppy looked anymore like a king than the Christ child must have in the manger.

"Does this mean we can keep him? I mean, keep King?" Hannah asked.

Theresa tried to act put out. "*If* you promise to take care of him, and *if* you keep your rooms clean every day, and *if* you continue to make good grades in school, we can probably keep him."

This set off a chorus of squealing while King drizzled his enticement on the kitchen floor.

"Yippee!" Tiger shouted. "This is the best Christmas ever!"

"Except that Daddy's in jail," Hannah reminded him.

"Oh yeah," Tiger said. "I didn't mean that part."

32

JASMINE HAD NO time to second-guess her decision about the Hammond case. Late Monday afternoon the Fourth Circuit responded to the notice of appeal and request for an expedited schedule that David Arginot had filed early Monday morning. Arginot called Jasmine to break the news.

"They want both sides to file briefs by the close of business on Wednesday," he said. "Oral argument will be Thursday at 2:00 p.m. They're obviously trying to have a decision out by Friday, before Christmas."

Jasmine knew things would move fast—but two days to write the brief! She nearly had to pick herself up off the floor. "How much progress have you made on the brief?" she asked.

Arginot grunted. "I had my hands full this weekend responding to media requests. I was lucky to get the notice of appeal done today."

"So nothing—you've done nothing on the brief?"

"I've done some research, Jasmine." Defensiveness crept into Arginot's tone. "I've been a little busy."

"What about the town? Do you know how they're coming?"

This brought a sarcastic laugh. "The town?" Arginot repeated. "As in Mr. Ottmeyer?" Another forced chuckle. "We couldn't even talk him into filing an expedited appeal."

"What?"

"Yeah. Ottmeyer said the town didn't have any real immediacy associated with its case. No town officials are in jail, and even if they got a decision late this week, they've already missed the opportunity to display the manger scene in the final weeks before Christmas this year."

"What if they got a reversal on Friday? Is he saying they wouldn't even try to set something up for Saturday night or Christmas Eve?"

"I think what he's really saying, Jasmine, is that he knows we're pushing for an expedited appeal, and he can just tag along with a lot less work than if he filed his own."

"That's just stupid."

"You want his cell phone number so you can tell him that?"

Jasmine sighed. "No. I've got too much work to do."

They spoke for a few more minutes about the details of the appeal, with Jasmine expecting Arginot to offer his help in some way on the brief. But there were apparently too many media opportunities still to mine. When she hung up the phone, one thing was blatantly obvious—she might have to share the credit if they won, but there was nobody willing to share the work in the meantime.

Forty-eight hours to write, edit, and file the most important brief of her life.

She found a study carrel in the back of the library, booted up her laptop, and settled in for a long night.

33

TUESDAY, DECEMBER 19

By Tuesday afternoon Jasmine started to panic. Twenty-four hours had passed since the phone call with Arginot. In another twenty-four hours she had to file her brief. That deadline had kept her at the library until it closed at midnight, when she shifted to her apartment, where she worked the rest of the night. Still, she was making little progress. She would write a few pages, throw them out, do some more research, then repeat the process. At this rate Thomas Hammond would lose by default.

The case seemed simple enough—can a town display a manger scene on the town square along with other symbols of the holiday season? That question had already been answered affirmatively by the Supreme Court. But the town and its attorney had fumbled this matter so badly that it was almost impossible to construct a good argument on behalf of Thomas.

If the town had initially included the manger scene as part of a much broader display of Christmas traditions, they would have been fine. The case would have been virtually identical to *Lynch v. Donnelly*, where the Court held that the crèche had a secular purpose—depicting the historical origins of a national holiday—and therefore didn't violate the establishment clause when it was displayed alongside other symbols of the season. But the original display in Possum had included only the manger scene, a Christmas tree, and an unmanned Santa Claus sleigh. And the display was managed by the mayor's own church, a fact that Harrod would undoubtedly emphasize to show that a reasonable observer would view it as an endorsement of the Christian religion.

The town's attempt to remedy the situation—Operation Xmas Spirit—had its own set of difficulties. According to Ichabod, Possum had shown its true religious purpose when it first displayed the crèche pretty much by itself. Judge Baker-Kline ruled that this original purpose tainted even the Operation Xmas Spirit display, despite the fact that the new display had more things secular than it did religious.

To make matters worse, Jasmine was not even sure that she could raise these issues about Ichabod's first two rulings on *her* appeal. Thomas was not in jail because of the original display or the Operation Xmas Spirit display—he was in jail because he kept setting up his own display. Under the *Capitol Square Review* case, Thomas should have been allowed to set up a religious display in a public arena using the same application and permitting process that everyone else had used. But that was the problem. Thomas hadn't been treated the same. He had been given preferential treatment and granted a permit only *after* he had already set up the crèche.

What a mess, Jasmine thought. She rubbed her eyes and stared at her laptop screen.

Her cell phone vibrated. Though she had made a rule not to answer any calls or check voice mail until she filed her brief, she glanced at the caller ID out of curiosity. Area code 212. Pearson Payne or some New York talk-show producer. It was the third time today someone had called from a New York City area code.

Jasmine let the call kick into voice mail and then, knowing she would regret it later, started checking her messages. There were eight, three from Pearson Payne. He didn't sound happy.

She rubbed her face and settled back to work, but she couldn't get her mind off the calls. You couldn't refuse to call back a man as powerful as Pearson Payne, though she really didn't want to deal with him right now. The publicity on the case had continued, with Christian leaders calling for spontaneous displays of manger scenes everywhere—church property, private homes, town squares. Jasmine was pretty sure that Reverend Hester was still using the controversy to raise boatloads of money, though she didn't have time to check.

Pearson would not be happy. But still, she owed him a call.

She grabbed her cell phone and walked outside the library into the frigid late-afternoon air. She knew that Pearson would still be in his office—New York firms get their second wind at 5 p.m. She dialed the number and closed her eyes.

"Pearson Payne's office."

"Hi, this is Jazz Woodfaulk returning Mr. Payne's calls."

"One moment please."

When Pearson came on the line, Jasmine braced for an explosion. Instead, Pearson asked about the case and seemed genuinely interested as Jasmine explained her predicament. He quizzed her about the hearings in front of Judge Baker-Kline and made a few suggestions about how to argue the appeal, mostly things Jasmine had already considered. She told him how panicked she was about filing a brief tomorrow that she hadn't really even started.

"Sounds like a loser, Jazz. You really ought to withdraw."

"I can't, Mr. Payne. Not now."

Pearson paused for a long time and Jasmine knew what was coming.

"Well, that's a call you've got to make. I admire your tenacity, you know that. And you'll have a great future at some law firm. But unfortunately, it won't be with us. It wouldn't be fair for me to bring you in here after this case. Half my partners would be gunning for you from day one. It's hard enough to make partner when you come in with a clean slate. Under these circumstances, you wouldn't stand a chance. And, Jazz, I like you too much to put you through that."

Though she saw it coming, the words still hit hard. "I understand, Mr. Payne. Thanks for being a straight shooter with me." Even as she spoke, Jasmine marveled at the great lawyer on the other end of the phone. *He* was revoking *her* job offer, but somehow he had *her* thanking *him*!

She heard a quick beep from his phone. "Jazz, I just got another call that I've got to take. Good luck on that appeal."

"Thanks, Mr. Payne."

"I'm sorry."

"I know."

She stared at the phone for several seconds before heading back into the library. First the WNBA and now New York City. But she didn't have time to feel sorry for herself. She could host a pity party later. She had a deadline less than twenty-four hours away.

34

WEDNESDAY, DECEMBER 20

It came in an e-mail a few minutes after ten . . . and it came none too soon. Jasmine had to blink twice before she opened it, still punchy from getting only a few hours' sleep on Tuesday night after none at all on Monday. She was in the midst of throwing her appellate brief together, a disjointed hodgepodge of ideas and cases that barely convinced her and certainly stood no chance of weathering the scrutiny of the Fourth Circuit. Despair had yielded to a grim determination to file something by the deadline, even if she would be embarrassed to attach her name to it.

She was in the library, hooked up to the school's wireless Internet, when the e-mail message flashed on her screen. Like phone calls, she had been ignoring her e-mails, but this one drew her like a tropical oasis after two long days in the desert.

The sender was Pearson Payne, but it might as well have been a direct delivery from heaven.

> As you know, we require a fair amount of pro bono work from our associates at Gold, Franks. And since we really aren't that busy right now, I asked a few of our best young guns to take a stab at drafting your appellate brief last night. Hope this helps. By the way, Scooter says hi.
>
> *Merry Christmas, Pearson Payne*

Adrenaline pumping, Jasmine double-clicked on the Word document. It was a twenty-five-page brief, properly formatted and edited to comply precisely with Fourth Circuit guidelines. The signature page contained a line for both Jasmine and Arginot. She wanted to kiss the laptop.

She skimmed past the index of authorities cited—lots of impressive-looking case law—and began reading.

> Issue Presented: Can a federal judge rule Christmas unconstitutional?
>
> Summary of Argument: In a prior case upholding the right of a city to display a manger scene, the Supreme Court noted that the First Amendment does not require total separation of church and state. The government's job is to accommodate religion, not eradicate it. "We are a religious people whose institutions presuppose a Supreme Being," the Court reminded us, quoting language from one of its own prior opinions upholding government-paid chaplains.

196

Our history is replete with references to our religious history and traditions: our national motto "in God we trust," the Pledge of Allegiance's "one nation under God," our national holidays, and the oath taken by every witness sworn in by our federal courts—"so help me God." As Justice Douglas once observed, accommodation toward all faiths, and hostility toward none, has honored "the best of our traditions" and "[respected] the religious nature of our people."

The issue here is whether a single federal judge can ignore centuries of tradition, along with a controlling opinion of the United States Supreme Court, and declare illegal a pivotal part of a time-honored national holiday. If the manger scene is illegal, can the Christmas holiday itself be far behind? Let's not pretend. Christmas is by its very nature religious, commemorating the birth of Jesus Christ, the central historical figure of the Christian faith. Under our Constitution, there's nothing wrong with that. The First Amendment does not require that federal judges replace a religious society with an atheistic one.

This court should reverse the Order of the District Court declaring the manger scene unconstitutional and thereby invalidate Mr. Hammond's contempt citation for failure to comply with that order. Our Republic has flourished despite Christmas celebrations and manger scenes for more than two hundred years. Or perhaps, in part, because of them.

It can certainly survive one more.

Jasmine stopped reading, inspired by the rhetoric. She had been so caught up in the details of the case that she had lost sight of the big picture. It took these New York lawyers, who probably didn't even believe in Christmas, to show her what was really at stake. They were right. This wasn't about how many secular symbols Possum put on its town square alongside a manger scene—the so-called three reindeer rule.

This case was about Christmas. Vote it up or down. That had to be her message to the Fourth Circuit. And it took an agnostic New York lawyer, who probably worked straight through Christmas himself, to reveal this to her.

She would finish reading the brief, sign it, deliver it, and get a few hours' sleep. But first she typed an e-mail to Pearson Payne, thanking him for what he had done.

I wish there was some way I could repay you, she wrote.

A few minutes later, she received his reply.

There is. Win the case.

35

THURSDAY, DECEMBER 21

At precisely 2:00 p.m. on Thursday, the three judges assigned to the Hammond case took their seats high on the dais and the clerk called the Fourth Circuit Court of Appeals to order. Jasmine took her position behind the podium, spread her materials in front of her, and grabbed both sides of the lectern. Within minutes she was fielding questions like a seasoned veteran.

Justice Otis Clarence, an African American Bush appointee who attended law school after a brief stint in the NFL, dominated the early questions. He pitched softballs at Jasmine, his bias evident for all to see.

"Why isn't this case controlled by *Lynch*?" he asked. "It

seems to me that just because the city in *Lynch* had a few more secular decorations around the crèche doesn't make its display substantially different from the one in Possum."

"I agree, Justice Clarence. The Court in *Lynch* said that the crèche depicts the historical origins of a national holiday. As such, it served a secular purpose, not a religious one."

Justice Langley Williams, a nerdy-looking judge well into his seventies, furrowed his brow. "Didn't *your client* say it had a religious purpose?"

"He doesn't speak for the town, Your Honor."

"But he does attend Sunday school with the mayor. And they did pray for people who visited the crèche."

"Which doesn't magically turn the crèche into a prohibited religious symbol," Jasmine shot back. She was trying hard not to sound defensive but was not entirely succeeding. "Mrs. Hammond is in that same Sunday school class and tells me that this week they're praying for this court to make the right decision. I prayed with my client before this hearing. Those prayers don't transform this court into an unconstitutionally religious body."

Williams scowled but apparently couldn't think of an immediate comeback. Jasmine had written him off anyway. A Carter appointee, Williams had never seen a religious symbol he didn't want to expunge from public property.

Jasmine paused long enough to emphasize that she had silenced Williams, then went for another nail in the coffin. "Even if you do find the crèche to be a religious symbol, that doesn't end the inquiry. The U.S. Supreme Court has long upheld symbols of ceremonial deism and religious practices associated with the fabric of our society. It's why we allow government-paid chaplains and religious holidays and In God

We Trust on our currency. It's why the Ten Commandments are still displayed as part of a frieze in the U.S. Supreme Court building. We are, after all, a nation steeped in religious tradition, and according to our own Declaration of Independence—"

Jasmine stopped midsentence when Justice Karen Sanders cleared her throat. Here was the swing vote—the elegant lady with the gray hair and wire-rimmed glasses sitting in the middle. "Counsel," she began, and it seemed the entire courtroom held its breath, "isn't all this talk about the secular or religious nature of the first two displays by the town irrelevant?"

Jasmine's knees trembled. "In what way, Your Honor?"

"Well, Ms. Woodfaulk, unless I'm missing something here, your client's not in jail because he took part in the manger scenes sponsored by the town. He's in jail because he set up his own private manger scene later, without a permit, even after Judge Baker-Kline told him not to. So why are we spending all this time worrying about whether the town's manger scene displays were constitutional or not?"

Jasmine felt her heart pounding in her ears. This was the swing vote! She couldn't fumble this answer.

"The court's order for Mr. Hammond to stay away from the town square was predicated on its prior rulings that the manger scene displays sponsored by the town were unconstitutional. If Judge Baker-Kline had ruled correctly in the first two hearings, there would have been no order barring Mr. Hammond from setting up a crèche in the town square and thus no contempt citation."

Sanders screwed her face into a skeptical mask, unnerving Jasmine with the uncanny resemblance to Ichabod.

"If ifs and buts were candy and nuts, we'd all have a merry Christmas," Williams said, but Jasmine ignored him. *Go back to sleep, you old codger.*

"Let me give you an analogy," Sanders said. "Let's assume that this is a domestic disturbance case. And let's assume that Mrs. Hammond lied to a police officer to get a restraining order issued against Mr. Hammond. If Mr. Hammond violated that restraining order and attacked Mrs. Hammond, are you going to argue that he shouldn't be held in contempt because the underlying restraining order was predicated on a lie?"

"No, Your Honor. But displaying a crèche on town property is hardly akin to beating your wife."

Sanders turned her head slightly sideways like she wasn't buying it.

Swing vote, Jasmine reminded herself. "It's more like 'fruit of the poisonous tree,'" Jasmine explained. "In a criminal case, if the police improperly obtain a confession and use that confession to obtain a search warrant, all the evidence from the search will be thrown out as 'fruit of the poisonous tree.' That's what these contempt citations are—fruit of an improper ruling by a district court judge on the constitutionality of Operation Xmas Spirit."

Sanders jotted some notes as Williams awoke from his half slumber and resumed his hostile questioning, starting with the case of *Allegheny County v. ACLU*, in which the Supreme Court ruled against a county that displayed a stand-alone crèche. When the red light came on nearly twenty minutes later, Jasmine was physically and emotionally drained.

She sat down at counsel table next to Theresa, who had made the trip to Richmond with her. "Good job," Theresa whispered.

"Thanks," Jasmine managed. But she was already critiquing herself. She didn't think she had convinced Sanders, and Jasmine knew Williams wasn't going her way. Plus, as she watched the smooth arguments by Harrod and the unflinching way he handled their questions, it didn't exactly buoy her spirits.

When Harrod finally sat down, the clerk reminded Jasmine that she had reserved two minutes for rebuttal. She rose to the podium, feeling a bit like a weary fighter coming off the stool for one last round. She tried to ignore the intimidating stare of Williams.

She had made a few notes during Harrod's argument but didn't take them to the podium. She could feel this hearing slipping away, two of the three judges possibly leaning against her. She needed to do more than bicker about fruit of the poisonous tree and how many Frosty the Snowman displays it took to neutralize one crèche. Her competitive instincts told her it was time to throw down the gauntlet and remind the judges of the big picture, the policy arguments so beautifully laid out in the brief drafted by Scooter McCray and reviewed by Pearson Payne.

This was about the right to celebrate Christmas, pure and simple.

"Merry Christmas, Your Honors. Godspeed. God bless you. So help me God." She paused, practically daring the justices to fire off a question. "This court is public property. Paid for by taxpayer dollars. Yet I've just invoked the name of the Almighty, heaven forbid, three separate times—four if you count Christ. Does Mr. Harrod believe we've just established a religion?"

Jasmine pulled her cross necklace from under the collar of her blouse for all to see. She was out on a limb now, might as well keep sawing. "I'm wearing this cross necklace. On government property, God forbid! And you're allowing it! Isn't that unconstitutional? And what about that silent prayer I said just before I stood up—should I be thrown in jail for that?" She turned and pointed toward a stunned Theresa. "And perhaps Mrs. Hammond is praying right now, wondering what in the world got into her bombastic lawyer—should *she* be held in contempt?"

Jasmine paused and pretended not to be bothered by the slack-jawed looks of the justices. "Where will it stop? How ironic that a country founded by those seeking religious freedom may now be telling its citizens freedom *from* religion will replace freedom *of* religion in the public square.

"Did the brave men who drafted the Constitution really intend to purge the public square of all things religious? Can anyone seriously argue that Washington, Jefferson, and Adams would have been offended by a crèche? Washington, who proclaimed the first day of national Thanksgiving by saying, 'It is the duty of all nations to acknowledge the providence of Almighty God'? Jefferson, who referenced God four times in the Declaration of Independence? Adams, who said, 'Our Constitution was made only for a moral and religious people. It is wholly inadequate to the government of any other'?"

Though Jasmine was just getting rolling, she noticed the red light pop on.

"Your time is up, Ms. Woodfaulk," Justice Williams announced.

"God help us," Jasmine replied.

The reporters scribbled the words with glee. Who could have hoped for a better headline?

36

JASMINE AND THERESA listened to Christmas music on the way home from Richmond, reminding Jasmine of how little Christmas spirit she had. In a few days the season would be over. Never before had Christmas snuck up on her so quickly. So much had happened recently—the implosion of her New York job, law school exams, this case falling apart, and the basketball mess involving Ajori. She had no time for Christmas. How ironic!

Just when she determined that she would get into the Christmas mood if it killed her, the radio started playing "We Wish You a Merry Christmas" and her Christmas resolve evaporated. She could no longer stand this song with its evil chorus demanding figgy pudding. She could picture the mobs going from house to house, demanding their pudding and looting any puddingless homeowners. Though Jasmine hadn't been in court the day Ichabod had taught her little history lesson about Christmas, she had reviewed the transcript in preparation for the appeal. She could imagine the smirk on Ichabod's face as she grilled Mayor Frumpkin about the origins of the song. "We Wish You a Merry Christmas" was turning Jasmine into Scrooge.

She hit a button and changed the station. "'Tis the Season to Be Jolly." *That's better,* she thought. She even started singing along a little in her mind until . . . "Don we now our gay apparel."

"You mind if we turn that off?" Jasmine asked.

"I was just thinking the same thing," Theresa said.

Jasmine thought about how much Christmas had changed for her. Growing up, she had loved the Christmas carols and traditions, the surprises under the tree, the "Merry Christmas" greetings from complete strangers in Possum, and the inevitable Christmas basketball tournaments. She had never understood those who said the Christmas season was one of the most stressful times of the year.

But losing her dad had changed a lot of that. Christmas traditions became searing reminders of the empty place at the table. Christmas tournaments weren't the same without her dad stalking the sidelines. And now, on top of all that, she had a client sitting in jail through Christmas Day unless they pulled out a miracle win at the Fourth Circuit. Jasmine found herself secretly wishing that Christmas was over.

Four more days, she told herself. Four more days.

★

When Jasmine arrived home early Thursday evening, she was immediately bombarded with questions from her mom and Ajori. "You were all over TV," Ajori announced. But Jasmine was tired of the case and all its pressures.

"Can we not talk about it?" she asked.

Bernice and Ajori exchanged a look. "Now you know how I feel after my games," Ajori said.

"Whatever."

Jasmine's mom tried to change the subject by talking about Christmas things, but that didn't work either. "I just can't get in the Christmas spirit," Jasmine confided. Saying it out loud actually sounded weird, like she had just confessed to some heinous crime or perhaps a psychotic delusion. What normal person couldn't get in the Christmas spirit?

Fortunately, Ajori had a solution. "Me neither. We need to get our sorry butts to the mall!"

By Ajori's hasty calculations, they could still get in a few hours of shopping if they left immediately. Since Ajori was now on Christmas vacation, it was a no-brainer. The girls guilt-tripped their mom into handing over her credit card, and they were off.

Jasmine received the call while riffling through the faded jeans in the Old Navy store. "Jasmine, it's Mr. Greenway. I got your cell number from your mom."

Jasmine shot a glance at Ajori, a few feet away looking at sweaters. Jasmine ducked her head and wandered toward the other side of the store. "Hey," she said. Though it seemed awkward not to say his name, she wasn't out of earshot of

Ajori yet and she was pretty sure she knew why Greenway was calling.

"Have you thought about my offer?" Greenway asked. "Barker tried to resign again after last Friday's fiasco."

"I really haven't had time to think about much of anything these last few days," Jasmine confessed. She was trying to casually walk away from Ajori, but her little sister had picked up the scent and was following her. "And that's the problem. I'm just so busy as it is. There's no way I could take on something else."

Greenway paused long enough to show his disappointment. "Is that a no, then?"

Jasmine sighed. For some reason, she couldn't quite bring herself to say it. Ajori was closing in, so Jasmine waved her off. This, of course, made Ajori move closer.

"I'm not a coach, Mr. Greenway," Jasmine said softly, turning her back on her little sister. "There's a big difference between being a player and a coach."

"You'd do great, Jazz. You were a natural the other night."

Jasmine started to object, but Ajori was hovering too close for her to say anything else that might give away this conversation. The last thing Jasmine needed was her little sister begging her to do this.

"Tell you what," Greenway continued. "How about if I have Barker drop some game films off at your mom's. You can watch the tapes of the first few games that you didn't see. You look at the game films tomorrow and ask yourself honestly if you could help this team. The Christmas tournament starts next week, so I'll need your decision by Saturday."

Jasmine kept one eye on Ajori. How could she phrase this? "What's the alternative?" she asked.

"I talk Barker out of quitting. Or talk Rebecca Arlington into taking over."

Jasmine closed her eyes. She could outcoach either of them in her sleep. "I'll come pick them up," she said.

"Pick what up—the tapes?"

"Yeah. Tomorrow. Is there someplace there I could watch them?"

"At the school?"

"Yeah."

"Sure. There aren't any students here, so I'll set you up in a classroom. Is Ajori listening to your end of this?"

"Yes, sir."

"I get it."

By now Ajori was giving Jasmine dirty looks. Prime shopping time was slipping away.

"Gotta run," Jasmine said.

"What time you coming by?" Greenway asked.

"Does nine work?"

"I'll be there."

37

A man who identified himself only as Santana Kringle shuffled toward the judge's bench, head down, hands cuffed behind his back. His long, matted gray bread covered most of his face but couldn't hide the red and bulbous nose, one of many signs that his body had processed enough alcohol for ten men. His hair receded and he wore it straight back, tucking the greasy gray strands behind his ears. His clothes, including a heavy wool coat, were grimy and tattered, faded to the color of the streets. His body odor arrived at the judge's dais a few seconds before Santana himself did.

The prosecutor stood beside him while a marshal loitered a few steps behind.

Judge Cynthia Baker-Kline looked at her docket sheet and smirked when she saw the name. Last month, the day before Thanksgiving, this same man had identified himself as John Pilgrim. "Is this man dangerous?" the judge asked the prosecutor. She was a new member of the U.S. attorney's staff, someone Judge Baker-Kline had seen only a few times before.

"I don't believe so, Your Honor."

"Then uncuff him."

As the marshal complied, Santana looked up.

"Good morning, Mr. Kringle."

"Good morning, Judge."

"You have the right to an attorney. If you can't afford one—"

"I'll waive it," Santana said.

"You know where to sign."

The prosecutor shoved some papers in front of the man, and he scribbled his signature. The prosecutor put the paper in her file and then began reading the charges. "Mr. Kringle is being charged with trespass on government property," she began. "The steps of this courthouse, Judge. We asked him to leave several times, but he refused."

"Guilty," Santana said.

The prosecutor looked stunned. Judge Baker-Kline smiled. "You want two days or three, Mr. Kringle?"

"What's the weather supposed to be like?" the defendant asked.

"Chance of rain or maybe even a little snow tomorrow," the judge said. "Supposed to warm up some on Christmas. Tuesday should be all the way up to the fifties."

"I'll stay through Christmas, Judge."

"Suit yourself." She banged her gavel. "I find the defendant guilty of trespass on government property and hereby sentence him to three days in the federal holding tank." She glanced back at the federal marshal. "Make sure he gets a turkey dinner on Monday."

She had issued the same order on Thanksgiving and on the same two holidays last year. For some reason, making sure that the Norfolk bum had a warm place to spend Thanksgiving and Christmas made her feel as good as any order she entered all year.

Santana smiled, showing rows of yellow teeth. "God bless you, Judge. The homeless shelter is pretty crowded this time of year."

"Merry Christmas," Judge Baker-Kline said.

★

By 11:00 a.m. Jasmine had watched two full games and taken nearly five pages of notes. She sat back in the chair and rubbed her tired eyes. She was getting caught up in this—she couldn't help it. Her sister's team wasn't that bad; certainly much better than their 1–7 record. They had the talent to beat most of these teams. All they needed was a change in philosophy and a little . . .

Stop! she told herself. *You're a law student, not a basketball coach. What are you even doing here?*

She looked at the videotapes on the desk, all labeled with the names of familiar schools. Each brought back memories of a certain gym with its own unique smell and feel, the different chants of the student bodies, the dead spots on the gym floors, silencing the other team's crowd, celebrating with teammates afterward. She wanted Ajori to have those same memories. But even if Jasmine was willing to sacrifice her last semester of law school, could she coach well enough to turn this team around?

One thing was sure, nothing could be worse than Barker.

Her mind wandered to the Hammond case. Everyone expected the appellate court to rule today, and Arginot had promised to call as soon as the opinion came down. If they won, Arginot would blanket the talk shows between now and Christmas morning while Thomas would probably be back out on the square on Christmas Eve. Jasmine allowed herself to linger there for a moment. How sweet would that be? A candlelight Christmas Eve service on the town square.

But if they lost? She couldn't allow herself to dwell on that.

She looked back at the pile of tapes, trying to decide which one to watch next, then smiled as her eyes landed on the tape of *Hoosiers*. It had been included with the other tapes left in this classroom for Jasmine to watch. There was a note attached to it: *I showed this one to the team for inspiration.*

That, in a nutshell, was Barker's problem—believing a movie like this would motivate girls today. The movie was about a dysfunctional Indiana high school basketball team from the fifties that nobody believed could win. A new charismatic coach, played by Gene Hackman, moved into town and rallied the team behind him. They ended up winning the state championship, beating teams from schools ten times their size in the process.

Jasmine had seen the movie—what basketball player hadn't?—but she knew it wouldn't motivate high school girls in the twenty-first century. She popped it in for fun, just to laugh at the short shorts with the little belts and the old-school set shots the players used. Jasmine was pretty sure that any half-decent girls' team from Possum's league could beat the team featured in *Hoosiers*. Times had changed . . . for everybody but Coach Barker.

The tape hadn't been rewound, but that was all right. Sure enough, the players all wore their skintight short shorts with long (and very white) legs sticking out the bottom. Tank tops were in, short hair was in, and the girls all wore bobby socks. What nonsense, trying to motivate Ajori's team with this.

Jasmine was now viewing a scene where the head coach in *Hoosiers* tried to get himself tossed out of the game so the assistant coach, a recovering alcoholic, would realize that he could coach all by himself and earn the respect of his son in the process. After a bad call, Hackman's character went toe-to-toe with the ref.

"You're pathetic, you know that?" Hackman yelled.

The ref tried to calm him down, but to no avail. "You're a disgrace to the profession!" Hackman screamed.

Jasmine sat up in her chair and leaned forward. *Pathetic. A disgrace to the profession.* Almost the exact words!

She watched as Hackman edged closer to the referee. "Throw me out," he said, nearly whispering.

"You're putting me on."

"Kick me out of the game or I'll start screaming like a mad fool."

The ref shrugged, said, "I guess you have your reasons," and tossed the coach out.

"What?" Hackman yelled. "That's ridiculous!" He sulked out of the gym, leaving his assistant to handle the team on his own, discovering in the process that he could actually coach.

Jasmine ejected *Hoosiers* and scrambled for the Franklin

High tape. She ran it on fast-forward until she found the place where Barker was ejected. Given the sparse attendance, it was not surprising that the camera picked up most of what Barker had said. "Unbelievable," she muttered. It was a carbon copy of *Hoosiers*, just with longer shorts worn by girls instead of guys. There was even a segment where Barker leaned in and said something to the ref, just before he got thrown out. Though she couldn't hear it, Jasmine was pretty certain what was said.

She shook her head at the discovery. She couldn't tell from the tape whether Barker had gotten himself thrown out so Rebecca Arlington could coach, or whether he somehow knew that Jasmine would step in. But one thing was clear—Barker intentionally instigated his own ejection as some warped attempt to groom a replacement.

Jasmine wasn't sure what to think as she called Greenway. "Who put these tapes together for me?" she asked.

"Coach Barker, as far as I know. I asked him to pull together the game tapes for your review and place them in that classroom. He didn't sound happy about it, but I think he came in early this morning."

"Is he still here?"

Greenway scoffed. "Jazz, it's the day before the Christmas weekend. There's nobody here but you, me, and one member of the janitorial crew."

"Dumb question." Jasmine thought for a moment. "What does Barker teach?"

"Psychology and sociology," Greenway replied. She could hear the curiosity in his voice. "Does that matter? We're not asking you to teach."

"Just checking." Jasmine heard the telltale beep that

indicated another call on her cell. She checked the number. "Can I call you right back?" she asked the principal. "I've got another call I need to take."

Arginot's name appeared on the screen, and she punched the button to answer. It was hard to even breathe, knowing that he might be calling with the Fourth Circuit's decision. "Hello."

"The clerk just announced that the Fourth Circuit will issue their opinion at 5:00 p.m. today," Arginot said. "They're going to post it on their Web site."

Jasmine relaxed, but only for a second. "That doesn't give us much time to appeal if we lose."

"Or for the other side if we win," Arginot responded. "Either way, I'll be ready. I've already investigated the best way to get a petition to the appropriate Supreme Court justice on Saturday if we have to."

"Good. But let's hope we don't have to."

They talked for a few more minutes, charting out plans for the worst-case scenario—an emergency appeal to the Supreme Court. It occurred to Jasmine how fortunate she was to still have Arginot involved in the case. At least he was admitted to the Supreme Court bar.

She hung up the phone and began worrying in earnest. The tapes no longer held any appeal.

★

After lunch, Judge Baker-Kline called her law clerk into her office. She handed the clerk a medium-sized box wrapped in brightly colored paper decorated with pictures of the Grinch, his heart bursting from his chest. The judge had written the name of Santana Kringle on the outside but no indication of whom the present was from. It was the same paper she had used for the gift she gave the clerk earlier that morning.

"I've got one more thing I'd like for you to do today, and then you can get an early start on the weekend," Judge Baker-Kline said. She had plans to stay until the Fourth Circuit opinion came down, but she would rather face it alone.

"Okay."

The judge handed the box to the clerk. "Could you take this to the jail? Make sure Mr. Kringle gets it when he leaves."

"Yes, ma'am," the clerk said. The judge could see the curiosity in the young girl's eyes, but politeness won out. "Anything else?" the clerk asked.

"No. That's it."

The clerk hesitated for a moment, apparently unsure of whether she should say anything about the upcoming Fourth Circuit's decision. "Merry Christmas, Judge. Have a great weekend."

"Merry Christmas."

Judge Baker-Kline bent over her papers and went back to work, thinking about how warm Santana would be in his new wool jacket.

38

JASMINE WORRIED HERSELF sick all afternoon. She skipped lunch, drove to her apartment in Virginia Beach, and weighed the scenarios—what to do if they won, what to do if they lost. She ignored phone calls and waited alone in her apartment, surfing the Internet and listening to Fox News. She wanted to digest the opinion alone, giving herself time to collect her thoughts before she sprang into action. Theresa was at the jail with Bernice's cell phone—waiting along with Thomas for a phone call from Jasmine.

Jasmine went to the Fourth Circuit site a few minutes before five, just in case, and then double-clicked on the icon for *Today's Opinions*. It loaded slowly, unusual for Jasmine's

DSL line. She double-clicked again and got an error message. Frustrated, she tried a third time. Another error message!

Argh! It was now 4:59. The opinion was either out or coming out, she had a client relying on her, and for some reason she couldn't access the site. She tried again. No luck. The heavy traffic from those who wanted to download the opinion must have crashed the site.

She picked up her cell and dialed Arginot. A recording. She cursed at her laptop. Then a Fox News reporter announced a breaking story.

She turned up the television and considered the irony. Here she was, counsel of record, learning the result just like every other American.

"Fox News has just learned that a sharply divided three-judge panel for the Fourth Circuit Court of Appeals has affirmed the order of District Judge Cynthia Baker-Kline. It appears that the man who has become known as the 'Crèche Crusader' will spend Christmas Day in jail."

Jasmine's heart dropped to her knees. She thought she was prepared for this, but her emotions started running away with her. She tried the Web site again. When it wouldn't load, she slammed her fist on the desk. *Is this justice?* she demanded of no one. They flashed some segments of the Fourth Circuit opinion on the screen, and Jasmine found herself seething at Judge Baker-Kline. How could the Fourth Circuit let her get away with this?

She flicked channels to see if she could learn more about the opinion. A CNN reporter was interviewing an attorney who babbled on about the precedent of the ruling. CBS was still running its regularly scheduled programming. But the ABC channel had interrupted for a special report—the reporter was actually interviewing Arginot on the steps of the courthouse. Arginot must have been waiting there so he'd look like a real lawyer for the television cameras.

"We'll appeal," Arginot promised. "We all knew that the Supreme Court would ultimately have to make this call. This is one battle, not the war."

"How quickly do you think the Supreme Court will rule?" a reporter asked.

"We can't say for sure." Arginot looked directly into the camera, the composure oozing from his tailored suit and overcoat. "But we're hoping for a Christmas miracle."

Jasmine scoffed and dialed her mom's cell phone number. She hated this part.

"Hello," Theresa Hammond said.

"We lost," Jasmine said. Dead silence filled the line. "I'm on my way over. We'll talk when I get there."

"Okay." Theresa's voice was thin, fragile. "I'll tell Thomas."

★

Thomas and Theresa listened intently as Jasmine explained the nuances of the opinion she had finally retrieved from the Fox News Web site. Theresa seemed close to tears, but Thomas showed no emotion. "I really wish the town had filed an expedited appeal along with us," Jasmine said. "The court took great pains to say, in a footnote, that this opinion did not mean the Fourth Circuit was affirming Baker-Kline's rulings against the town's manger scene display. In fact, let me read you their exact language." Jasmine thumbed through a few pages.

"Today's opinion is limited to the issue of whether Mr. Hammond had a constitutionally protected right to erect his own manger scene, with no other symbols of the Christmas holiday, on the town square. This opinion does not address whether the town's prior displays were constitutional or not. It would appear to this court on first blush that the secular nature of the town's Operation Xmas Spirit display is equivalent to the display upheld by the Supreme Court in *Lynch v. Donnelly*. But the town did not request an expedited appeal, and this court does not give advisory opinions. Resolution of the constitutionality of the town's displays will be decided on another day, after full briefing and argument before the court."

Jasmine stopped reading and looked into the puzzled eyes of her clients.

"What's that mean?" Thomas asked.

"It's the way appellate courts drop major hints," Jasmine explained. "They're basically saying that Judge Baker-Kline was right to hold you in contempt because she couldn't allow someone to display a manger scene all by itself, especially if he hadn't followed the right permitting procedures. But they're also saying that when the town appeals, we can probably expect a different result, since the town's displays had a variety of Christmas symbols in addition to the manger."

"Can we appeal to the Supreme Court?" Theresa asked.

Jasmine hesitated. "Typically, you would appeal a decision of a three-judge panel to the Fourth Circuit sitting *en banc*—"

Her clients looked confused. "That's all eleven judges of the Fourth Circuit sitting together," she explained. "But given the time constraints, Arginot wants to go directly to the Supreme Court. The problem is this: even if they decide to hear the case—and that's no guarantee—I just don't see any way we could get a ruling before Christmas."

At this news Theresa teared up and Thomas put his hand on top of hers. "Do you think we'll win if we appeal to them?" he asked.

"We might win. But the odds are against us. And if we lose, we establish a bad precedent for the whole country, not just the Fourth Circuit."

"So what are you suggesting?" Theresa asked.

"I think we should appeal," Jasmine said. "I just want you to know the downside."

"But you think the town's appeal, whenever that is heard, has a pretty good chance?" Thomas asked.

"Yes."

"So they could establish some good law in this same court . . . in this same circuit or whatever."

"Right."

"And maybe go up to the Supreme Court and establish some good law for the whole country?"

"It's possible," Jasmine said. "But there's never a guarantee that the Supreme Court will even take the case."

Thomas thought about this for a moment. "It seems obvious to me," he said. "We don't appeal. I serve my time through Christmas, and then we let the town appeal instead. They've got the strongest case—right?"

"Yes," Jasmine answered. "But they've . . ." She trailed off. How could she diplomatically explain that the town had the weakest attorney? "It's not either/or, Thomas. I think we should both appeal. We'll get two bites at the apple."

"But you said yourself we might establish some bad law."

"Yes, but—"

"I'm not interested in establishing any more bad law," Thomas said, squaring up his jaw. "I've seen what the courts think about Christmas. And I think I've made my point. We aren't going to appeal any further."

Jasmine didn't know what to say. Theresa stared at the table, and Thomas put on his stubborn mule face. "Okay," Jasmine said. "Why don't you sleep on it tonight? If you still feel that way in the morning, we won't appeal."

Thomas shook his head. "I don't need to sleep on it, Jasmine. You've done your level best. And I, for one, appreciate it. But we ain't gonna appeal."

Jasmine turned to Theresa. "You agree?"

She squeezed her husband's hand and nodded.

"Okay," Jasmine said. "I'll call Arginot and let him tell the world."

"Good," Thomas said. The three of them sat there in silence for a few moments, letting the finality of their loss hit home.

"It seems like such a shame," Theresa said.

And they all nodded in silent agreement.

39

CHRISTMAS EVE

Theresa opened her eyes and knew she wouldn't be going back to sleep. She awoke with that familiar sinking feeling in the pit of her stomach, the loneliness of missing Thomas. Still, she couldn't resist a small smile when she noticed the furry little ball curled up next to her in bed.

The first few nights King had slept in the crate, but he was a world-class whiner, and Theresa didn't have the heart to ignore the puppy's crying. On night three, Theresa allowed King to sleep in the bed with her, placing a rawhide bone by her feet, which King chewed on until he dozed off. Last night, she had done the same thing, but somehow the little

225

bugger had migrated up to the top of the bed and made a comfy home on Thomas's pillow.

Theresa reached over and scratched King behind his ears. "Don't get too comfortable there. One more night and that pillow will be spoken for."

As she took King outside to do his business, Theresa reflected on all that faced her the rest of the day. She and Thomas had talked last night and agreed on a plan. Thomas had insisted that they not come see him today. Theresa could bring the kids to the jail on Christmas, but Christmas Eve would go on as it always did. Following the Hammond family traditions would be important to the kids, especially now. Thomas said it would send a message: all the federal judges in the world couldn't keep Christmas from coming or the Hammond family from celebrating it.

Theresa wasn't interested in sending messages. She just wanted the kids to be happy. She just wanted to *survive* Christmas.

When the kids woke up, they would eat breakfast, dress warmly, go to church, and then go with Theresa to pick out their Charlie Brown Christmas tree. This tradition started two years ago, on Christmas Eve, when the family walked by the rejected trees in the Food Lion parking lot. Softhearted Hannah started feeling sorry for the trees and wondered what would happen to them if nobody picked them. Though they already had one tree, she talked her daddy into rescuing another one—the sorriest-looking tree on the lot. They put it in their already-cramped living room next to the first tree and decorated it with a few candy canes. You had to turn sideways to walk through the room.

Last year, their first Christmas in Possum, the family

decided to wait and get its one and only tree on Christmas Eve, picking out the motliest little tree still remaining in the town. Thomas used it as a teaching lesson: *This is what Christ does for us when nobody else thinks we're worth anything.* Theresa liked it because the tree was in the trailer for only a week and didn't shed nearly as many needles.

This year they would be picking the Charlie Brown tree without Thomas.

The rest of the morning would be spent decorating the tree and making Christmas cookies. Later the kids would help her deliver the cookies to a select list that included, for the first time this year, at Thomas's insistence, Judge Cynthia Baker-Kline.

Finally, tonight, the most important Christmas tradition of all: the reading of the Christmas story from the book of Luke. Theresa already knew this would be an emotional time. Watching in past years as the kids crawled into Thomas's lap and sat absolutely still while he read the familiar story of the Virgin Birth always made the rest of the hectic day seem worthwhile. This year, she just wanted to finish the story without crying.

It was a busy day, but she had carefully choreographed every minute of it and felt she had a reasonable chance of getting everything done. Like a good soldier, Theresa checked her list of logistics and supplies. She flicked on the television to catch a weather report and walked back into the kitchen to fix a pot of coffee, her only moment of relaxation before she jumped into this superhectic day.

And that's when she stepped in it. A small pool of yellow liquid in the middle of the linoleum floor.

"King!" she barked.

The little puppy peeked around the corner, slimy rubber ball in mouth, tail wagging, ready to play.

At least he's learning his name, Theresa thought.

40

AFTER A WARM lunch, Santana Kringle, badly in need of a nap, headed back to his cell. Though it was technically the inmates' recreation time, when they could hang out in the common area of the cell block to smoke cigarettes and watch television, Santana needed some rest. Of all the luck, he had drawn Thomas Hammond—*the* Thomas Hammond—as a cellmate. Santana had no issue sharing a cell with someone as notorious as Thomas. Thomas was a lot better than some of the crackheads who populated this joint. But there was one major problem.

The man snored like a freight train.

Santana thought he could sleep anywhere and through anything. Park benches, sewer grates, alcoves of buildings—they all worked fine as beds. Car horns, loud music, sirens—none of it kept Santana from getting his shut-eye.

But this! This was different. Hammond's snoring was not just loud, but sporadic. And it came from deep in the man's sinus cavity, like an underground explosion that would rattle to the surface and erupt in a snort of enormous proportions, shaking the cell-block walls and echoing back again.

About 4:00 a.m., Santana had become so desperate that he thought about climbing down from the top bunk, sneaking up next to Thomas, and kissing him gently on the cheek. He might get himself punched, but at least it would stop the snoring. Thomas would have one eye open the rest of the night, staying on guard against another kiss.

A few minutes after Santana hatched the plan, just moments before he crawled from his bunk to give Thomas the kiss, Santana fell asleep. But he knew he couldn't possibly go through that routine again tonight.

So now, as Santana rested on the top bunk and heard Thomas flipping the pages of his Bible, Santana decided on a new approach.

"How's it goin'?" he asked.

"Huh? Uh, good, I reckon. How 'bout you?"

"A little tired," Santana said.

Thomas grunted. "I didn't keep you awake with my snorin' last night, did I?"

"Nah. It's just hard to sleep when you're spending Christmas in jail away from your family."

"I hear that."

For the next several minutes, Santana dangled the bait. He got Thomas to talk about Theresa and Hannah and Tiger and Elizabeth, their Christmas traditions, and the looks on the kids' faces when they unwrapped their Christmas gifts. After an appropriate stroll down memory lane, Santana veered the conversation around to the matter at hand.

"Rumor has it you could be home with your kids tonight if you wanted to be."

Thomas hesitated. "Not without signin' a piece of paper that violates my conscience."

Santana sat up, legs hanging over the side of the bed. "What's the paper say?"

Thomas sighed and began explaining the saga of the manger scene. Santana grunted here and there to show he was listening, though he already knew exactly why Thomas was in jail. Living on the street, you had plenty of time to read the newspapers.

"Let me ask you a question," Santana said, after Thomas completed his version of events. "If you got out tonight, would you go set up a manger scene on the town square or spend tonight with your family?"

"Probably just spend it with Theresa and the kids."

"Exactly. So why not just sign the paper promising you won't set up the manger scene and go home? I mean, you probably wouldn't set up the manger scene even if you could."

"It's a matter of principle. I won't let that judge take away my constitutional rights."

Santana snorted as if constitutional rights were highly overrated. Then a new thought hit him—something that wasn't in the original script but just might work. "What's Christmas all about?" he asked.

"Huh?"

"What's Christmas all about?"

"Well, to a lot of people it's about shoppin' or family. But to me, it's about the Virgin Birth, Jesus coming to earth as a baby."

"Comin' from where?"

"Heaven, 'course—the right hand of God," Thomas answered.

I couldn't have planned this any better, Santana thought. "And you don't think He gave up any of His rights?" he asked. "That's the whole message of the Christmas season. Sometimes ya gotta give up a few rights to bring peace on earth."

This brought a prolonged silence from Thomas. "That's different."

"How?"

"I dunno. It just is."

This temporary setback was followed by another period of silence. Santana used it to think up a new approach. It wasn't easy thinking so hard without his daily dose of booze.

"Got a cigarette?" he asked.

"Nope."

"Didn't think so."

He thought for another moment and then real inspiration hit. "Who'd you say that judge was again?"

"Baker-Kline."

"Huh. I'd have never thought it."

"What?"

"You sure it was Baker-Kline?"

"Yeah. I'm sure."

Santana snorted his disbelief. "I thought she was one of the good guys."

"Whadya mean?"

"You know, that Bible case a couple years ago."

"Bible case?"

"You don't know about that?" Santana asked. He said it as if maybe Thomas had been living on Mars or something.

"I don't think so."

Santana climbed down from the top bunk and leaned against the bed. He wanted to look Thomas in the eye when he told him about the Bibles.

"Couple years ago, I was servin' some time on a bogus charge and got involved in a Bible study in here. Well, needless to say, I soon came to Jesus or found religion or whatever you want to call it. What I know is—something changed." He thumped his chest. "In here.

"Anyway, the Bible study was goin' gangbusters, and for some reason the guards shut it down. Well, one of my buddies files some kind of habeas petition and it gets assigned to Baker-Kline. Not only did she order the guards to let us have our Bible study, but she also bought Bibles herself for any inmate who didn't have one."

A dumbfounded Thomas stared at Santana in disbelief. It was clear that Santana was describing a different judge than the one Thomas knew. The old man swallowed hard and managed to choke back a tear or two. He looked away from Thomas toward the wall. "I'll never forget that," he continued, his voice thick. "And you wouldn't believe how much grief she took. All the liberals had a hissy fit. Tried to get her impeached."

"For real?" Thomas asked.

"Darndest thing about it," Santana continued as if he hadn't heard, "is that not one big-shot Christian came to her

233

defense. They made her take all that heat alone." He shook his head, saddened by the memory.

"How ironic that now she's gettin' blasted by all these Christians—I don't mean you, but the leaders out there, sayin' terrible things in the press. Well, anyway, darned if you do and darned if you don't." Santana took a glance at Thomas and then slowly headed out to the common area to give the big guy some time alone to think. "Guess I'll go see if I can find a cigarette."

Thomas grunted something, and Santana walked away smiling to himself. The thought of Baker-Kline giving out Bibles tickled him. Some kids needed to believe in Santa, and some adults needed to believe in benevolent judges. Santana was more than willing to indulge their fantasies. Whatever it took for a good night's sleep.

41

THE TEMPERATURE HOVERED around thirty-five degrees, dashing hopes for a white Christmas. The rain ended mid-afternoon, but the damp wind kept blowing, creating a wind-chill in the twenties. It would have been a good night to stay home, but Theresa and the kids were delivering the Christmas cookies they had decorated earlier. They'd done this for years, and some of their best friends now expected them—waiting with a cup of hot chocolate or some Christmas cookies of their own. All told, they had visited eight homes and now were just a few minutes away from their last stop, a Virginia Beach address.

Tiger had made sure all the broken cookies and the ones with sloppy icing ended up in this batch for Judge Cynthia

Baker-Kline, the woman who had put his daddy in jail. He thought he did it without his mom noticing, but Theresa knew exactly what Tiger was up to. Not that she was going to change it, of course, but still, it didn't go unnoticed.

Theresa checked her handwritten directions again and took a left. It was nearly seven o'clock, the clouds were blocking the stars, and Theresa had never been down this road before. She wished now that she had come here first and delivered these cookies while it was still daylight.

"Are we almost there?" Tiger asked from the backseat. "I gotta tinkle."

"You shoulda tinkled at the Pattersons' house," Hannah said, reading Theresa's mind.

"I didn't have to go then," Tiger said.

"Do you want me to pull over?" Theresa asked. She glanced over her shoulder—Elizabeth was sleeping in her car seat, and Tiger had his nose to the window.

"I'll hold it," he said.

Theresa slowed down and did her best to read mailbox numbers. This was the judge's road all right—a dark road that wound in front of large houses near the Lynnhaven River. The judge had some serious bucks. Each house had a set of stone or brick pillars bordering its driveway, guarding the estate like sentinels. The houses themselves were set back from the road a few hundred yards or more, the massive front lawns separating the privileged landowners from the masses who drove by. Though most of the lawns had tasteful Christmas lights twinkling in the trees and outlining the houses, they still seemed to scream *Keep Out!* to Theresa.

She read the number on a mailbox. "That's it," she said as cheerfully as possible. She turned in to the long driveway that curved for about a quarter of a mile through some pine and maple trees. When the driveway straightened out, she could see the stately brick home immediately in front of them. A dozen or more maple trees in the front yard were adorned with white lights on virtually every branch, the trunks trimmed in green. Two large elms, by contrast, had red lights on their trunks. White icicle lights traced the entire roofline of the house, and a large Christmas tree could be seen through the front picture window.

"It's beautiful," Hannah said.

"It looks like a haunted mansion to me," Tiger said.

"Tiger."

"It does," he said defensively.

Fortunately, the driveway circled right in front of the house. Though there were a few cars parked on each side, Theresa was pretty sure she could squeeze her minivan through, drop the cookies on the porch, and make a clean getaway. She thought for a moment about turning off her headlights so they wouldn't shine in one of the front windows and give her presence away. But then she thought about how lame that would look if she got caught.

She stopped right in front of the house and handed the plate of cookies, all wrapped up in aluminum foil, to Hannah. "It's kinda late," Theresa said. "And it looks like the judge has company. So why don't you just drop these on the front porch and then hop back in the van?"

"Should I ring the doorbell?" Hannah asked.

Theresa thought about this for a moment. Ringing the doorbell might bring somebody to the door right away. Then they would invite Theresa and the kids in. How awkward would that be?

"No," Theresa said. "No sense interrupting. She'll find them as soon as her company leaves."

"Okay," Hannah said. She grabbed the plate, climbed out of the van, placed the cookies carefully next to the doormat, then looked over her shoulder at Theresa. After Theresa nodded, Hannah tiptoed back to the van and gently closed her door.

"Go, Mom!" Tiger yelled. "Let's get outta here!" But he could have saved his breath. Theresa already had the minivan rolling down the driveway.

She checked the rearview mirror just before the driveway curved and the house went out of sight. Theresa thought she saw someone standing in the big front window, and then she saw the inside light go off.

★

Cynthia Baker-Kline started this Christmas Eve tradition about five years ago. When you're an only child, recently divorced, and you've just put your mom in a nursing home, you've got to do something different. Her dad had passed away four years before that, leaving behind the house and enough money to take care of the premises and her mom. To avoid confronting her loneliness, the judge invited four lawyer friends—all divorcées with grown children—to an elaborate Christmas Eve dinner. It was bring your own bottle of wine, and over the years, the competition for the most exotic and expensive wine had become fierce. Judge Baker-Kline had no chance of winning the competition on her government salary, so in year three, the hostess was granted an exemption from providing wine and was instead made a permanent wine-tasting judge.

She was in the kitchen, fetching another set of wineglasses for the next vintage bottle, when Ollie heard something outside and headed for the front door. The judge followed close behind.

She reached the foyer and peered out the glass panel next to the front door. She saw the minivan heading quickly down the drive. She stepped into the formal room and turned off the light so she could get a better look. The vehicle disappeared into the night. But the fates were with her. The right taillight was out.

She immediately dialed the federal marshals assigned to give her protection. Despite some recent death threats, she had refused a twenty-four-hour watch. Now she wondered if she had done the right thing.

The marshal on call said that the judge and her dinner guests should sit tight. A local patrol car would be dispatched to search the premises. A description of the vehicle—a minivan with a missing taillight—would be provided to Virginia Beach's finest. If he heard anything, he'd call her back immediately.

42

After making a clean getaway from the judge's house, Theresa put in the kids' favorite Christmas cassette. Before long they were singing at the top of their lungs to "Rudolph the Red-Nosed Reindeer"—all but Elizabeth, who sucked hard on her pacifier and kicked excitedly. The minivan rocked gently along, its driver oblivious to the police cruiser pulling up behind her until she saw the lights flash in her rearview mirror! Theresa immediately hit the power button on the cassette player. Only Tiger's squeaky little voice continued. "'He'll go down in . . .' Uh-oh!"

Theresa checked the speedometer—forty-seven. Just a few miles per hour over the posted speed limit. And it was almost Christmas for goodness' sakes! She slowed gradually, found a parking lot, and pulled over.

"What's wrong, Mommy?" Hannah fretted.

"Are we going to jail?" Tiger asked.

"No. Everything's fine," Theresa assured them.

"I'm scared," Hannah said.

"There's nothing to be scared of. The police are our friends," Theresa replied.

"Then how come they put Daddy in jail?" Tiger asked.

There was no time to explain. The cop was walking toward her car, shining a flashlight as bright as the sun in the windows. Theresa squinted as he pointed it in her face.

"License and registration, please."

She fished around in the glove compartment, whispered, "It's okay" to Hannah, and handed over the paperwork. The officer checked it for a moment, then flashed the light around the inside of the van again.

"Everything all right, Officer?" Theresa asked.

"Did you know you've got a taillight out?" the officer asked gruffly.

Theresa breathed a big sigh. So that's what this was all about. "No, sir, I didn't."

"You and the kids just drivin' around?"

Theresa tensed again. "No, sir. We were delivering some Christmas cookies."

"Christmas cookies, huh?"

Theresa nodded.

"Any place in particular?" the officer wanted to know.

"No, sir. Just some friends."

"Any judges' houses?"

Theresa stiffened. This must be the way criminals felt

when they got busted. But what had she done? Why should she act so ashamed?

"Yes, sir. We just delivered a batch to Judge Cynthia Baker-Kline."

"Christmas cookies." He said it with an arrogance that made Theresa want to scream.

"Yes, sir. The kids and I iced them ourselves." Theresa turned and looked at Tiger, who was nodding his affirmation like a little madman in the backseat. Even Elizabeth's eyes seemed wide with fear.

"Wait here," the officer said. Then he walked back to his car, taking her license and registration with him.

Elizabeth started fussing, and Theresa reached back to calm her while the officer wrote on a clipboard in the front seat of his car and talked on his car radio. Several minutes later he came back to Theresa's window.

"This is a ticket for improper equipment," he said. "You need to sign right here. If you get it fixed before your court date, the judge will probably drop the charge."

Theresa signed the ticket and resisted the urge to say a sarcastic "Merry Christmas."

"One other thing," the officer said. "You need to follow me back to the judge's place."

★

When Theresa pulled up in front of Judge Baker-Kline's, the judge was waiting on her front porch. She had on a long winter coat, pulled up at the collar, and her hands were jammed deep in the pockets. She walked over to the driver's door of the minivan, and Theresa rolled down her window.

"Hi," Judge Baker-Kline said.

"Hello, Your Honor," Theresa replied. It sounded dumb, but she didn't know what else to call her.

"It's Cynthia, please."

Theresa tried to smile. "Sorry."

"Thanks for coming back," the judge said. "I just wanted to apologize for getting you pulled over—"

"Oh, it's nothing," Theresa interrupted.

"No, it is. And it's incredibly thoughtful of you all to bring the cookies." She bent down and peeked at the kids. She smiled a little—the first time Theresa had seen that. "Hey, guys. Thanks for the cookies."

Tiger waved.

"You're welcome," Hannah said.

Theresa felt so uncomfortable. What did you say to the woman who put your husband in jail? Merry Christmas?

Judge Baker-Kline apparently felt uncomfortable too. She glanced at the ground. "I can't believe you brought the cookies . . . after everything you've been through. And then to get pulled over . . ." She paused, searching for words. "It's just that I've gotten a few threats lately, so security's pretty tight."

Threats? It had never occurred to Theresa that the judge might be having a tough time too. She thought about some of the things people said about her, even at church, and suddenly felt ashamed.

"I'm sorry, Your Honor."

"Oh . . . it's not your fault."

Another awkward silence fell between them as conflicting thoughts bombarded Theresa. How many times had she thought about giving this woman a piece of her mind? *Why*

do you have to be so mean-spirited? so haughty? so disrespectful of Christians? But here Theresa was—in a perfect setting to do it—and all she could feel was . . . sympathy?

"Well, good night," Judge Baker-Kline said. "And thanks again."

"You're welcome," Theresa said.

"You're welcome," the kids echoed.

As the judge turned toward the house, the front door opened and another woman appeared with a phone in her hand. "Telephone, Cynthia," she said.

Theresa placed the minivan in drive and started rolling up her window as the little guy burst through the judge's front door. A beautiful light brown and white cocker spaniel! He ran toward the judge, tail wagging, then darted away just before he got to her feet.

"Ollie!" she yelled. But he was already circling around the yard. The judge glanced at the van. *"Gol-ly!"* she said quickly, but she was not fooling Theresa. "That dog is impossible to catch!" It looked like she was blushing. "I'll have to go get a treat to bribe him back in the house."

"I'm sorry," the judge's visitor called from the front doorway. "I forgot about Ollie."

Hannah was up on her knees, watching wide-eyed as the dog stopped running and started sniffing around the front yard. "He looks just like King!" she said. She looked out Theresa's window at the judge. "What's his name?" Hannah asked.

Judge Baker-Kline hesitated a second too long. "His name is Spot," she said. "C'mere, Spot," she called. But the little cocker spaniel ignored her.

"Who wants a treat?" the judge yelled.

This time the dog lifted his head and sniffed in the general direction of the house. "Let's go get a treat!" she suggested, and the cocker spaniel started jogging toward her.

Theresa had been too stunned to move as she watched the scene unfold. But as dog and owner headed up the front steps, she felt like she had to say something.

"Merry Christmas!" Theresa yelled.

The judge turned and looked over her shoulder. "Merry Christmas, Mrs. Hammond." Then she headed inside to get Oliver Wendell Holmes the treat he so richly deserved.

43

It was a Woodfaulk family tradition—opening one gift on Christmas Eve—though Jasmine's dad used to put up token resistance, saying that opening the gift early showed a lack of discipline. But the kids would beg, Bernice would argue, and eventually they would all wear him down. Now it didn't seem quite the same; half the fun for Jasmine had been beating her dad into submission.

The three Woodfaulk women huddled on the couch next to the Christmas tree. Ajori began by lifting and shaking all the gifts with her name on them. "I'm going to open this one," she announced, holding up a box just big enough to hold a pair of jeans and a cute blouse she had been dropping major hints about. The gift was marked from *Santa*, a code word for her mom.

"No, you're not," Jasmine said. "I want you to open this one." She thrust a much smaller box at Ajori and watched her little sister try to disguise her disappointment. "This one's from me," Jasmine announced proudly.

"That's why I want to save it for tomorrow. You know, save the best for last."

"Nice try. But I really want you to open it tonight."

Ajori reluctantly set down the present she was holding and took Jasmine's, as if opening the gift from her sister was a major chore.

"Don't act so excited," Jasmine said.

"It's not that. It's just that I like saving the surprises until Christmas—I already know what's in this other box from mom."

The girls talked their way through it and soon had a plan. Bernice would go first, opening a present from the girls. Then Jasmine would open her present from Ajori. Last, Ajori would open Jasmine's present.

Bernice tore into the wrapping paper, then oohed and aahed over the cross necklace that matched the one Jasmine had worn to the Fourth Circuit argument. Bernice had been forbidden from attending—"I'm nervous enough as it is," Jasmine had said—but nearly burst with pride when she heard about her daughter's stunt.

"It's beautiful," Bernice gushed, and she put it on immediately.

Jasmine was up next, but Ajori made her sister try to guess before she could unwrap the odd-shaped package.

"Jeans?"

"Nope."

"A new coat?"

"Nope."

"Workout sweats?"

"You're not even warm. Think legal."

"Keys to a brand-new Porsche Carrera so I can ride in style while I look for a new job?"

Ajori scowled. "Don't you think it's a little big for car keys?"

"Sometimes you wrap them inside bigger stuff just to fool me."

Ajori shook her head.

Jasmine took her time, taking special care not to rip the paper, in an effort to drive her little sister nuts.

"Hurry up, grandma," Ajori said.

This slowed Jasmine down even more, but eventually she peeled the paper back. "A new backpack!" she exclaimed.

"Your old one looked a little ratty for court," Ajori said.

Jasmine didn't have the heart to tell her that real lawyers used briefcases. "Thanks." She gave Ajori a quick hug. "Now maybe I can win some cases."

"I don't know," Ajori said. "It's not magic."

Jasmine punched her sister on the arm.

"Mom!" Ajori whined.

Bernice rolled her eyes.

Ajori picked up her present, rattled it a little, then began guessing. "Socks? Victoria's Secret? Bath & Body Works? Coal?"

"Just open it," Jasmine said. "You'll never guess."

Ajori didn't have to be told twice. She ripped into the

paper, and her smile turned into a furrowed brow. "Ankle weights?"

"You wear them around all the time except when you're playing," Jasmine explained. "They'll increase your ups."

Ajori looked skeptical if not downright disappointed. "I know what to do with 'em, but they're so old-school. Nobody uses these anymore. They're bad for the knees."

"Well, you need to start using them," Jasmine insisted.

Ajori stiffened. Jasmine could tell her sister wanted to argue the point, but it was Christmas Eve, so she shrugged instead. "Hey, I'll try anything. Thanks, Jazz." She leaned over and gave her a quick hug.

"You'll do more than give them a try," Jasmine said. "If I'm gonna coach this team, my little sister needs to work on her ups."

Ajori's jaw dropped, and Jasmine's mom put her hands over her mouth, speechless. "What did you say?" Ajori managed.

"I said, if I'm going to coach this team—"

"Hold up!" Ajori shouted. "Stop right there—rewind. Are . . . you . . . *serious*?"

"Yep."

Ajori squealed and gave her sister another hug, this time with feeling.

"What about law school?" Jasmine's mom asked.

"I'm going to take a semester off and finish this summer." Jasmine searched her mom's face, looking for signs of approval. "When I pass the bar, I'll open up shop in Possum as a lawyer-coach. If that guy on TV can be a lawyer and run a bowling alley, I can certainly be a lawyer and a coach."

"Awesome!" Ajori shouted. "You rock!" She jumped up

and started pacing, then sat down and furiously laced on her ankle weights. "This is so cool! Wait till I call my friends. This is the best present ever! Has anyone seen my phone? I can't even believe this!"

While Ajori raved, Jasmine locked eyes briefly with her mom. Her mom was a little teary-eyed and wearing one of those tight-lipped smiles that moms get when their kids made them proud.

"You knew, didn't you, Mom?"

Bernice nodded with her whole body.

"How'd you know?"

"Moms know everything," she said.

"Then where's my phone?" Ajori asked.

Bernice rolled her glistening eyes. "Okay, maybe not everything."

A few minutes later, while Ajori worked the phone lines, Bernice disappeared for a moment and then came back downstairs with a small box wrapped in shiny silver paper.

"One more present tonight," she said while Ajori was between calls. "I wrapped it earlier but left it in my bedroom. Just in case."

"Who's it for?" Ajori asked.

"Well, it's got Jasmine's name on it. But it's really for both of you."

With Ajori on one side and her mom on the other, Jasmine unwrapped the small box. For some reason—maybe it was the seriousness of her mom's tone of voice—Jasmine felt her hands shaking. She pulled the small top off the box and felt her body go limp. "Oh, my goodness!"

She looked to her mom, then to Ajori, then back to the

precious small item in the box. She carefully picked up the string and pulled it out.

"Your dad's whistle," Bernice said as Jasmine gingerly placed the string around her neck. "I think he would want you to have it."

Jasmine held the chewed plastic whistle carefully between her thumb and forefinger as if someone had just placed the Hope diamond on her. She felt tears pooling in her eyes, but she didn't care. She could hear him again, blowing the whistle and yelling at her in practice. She could see him again, winking at her during games. "Take that chump to the rack," he'd say, patting her on the backside after a time-out. "She can't stop you!"

Jasmine wrapped her fist tight around the whistle. She closed her eyes and leaned back on the couch. She could feel her mom's arm on her shoulder and Ajori's hand on top of hers. And somewhere out there, Jasmine knew, her dad was smiling, pointing at her like he did when she made a good play. Thumping his chest, telling her that she had heart.

She loved the sound of that deep, deep voice. Soothing. Confident. Proud. *"That's my girl,"* he was saying. *"That's my girl."*

44

Elizabeth had fallen asleep on the way home. Theresa was proud of herself for having the other kids in bed by nine. She had read the Christmas story from the book of Luke, they had said their prayers, and she had fetched two glasses of water for Tiger, leading to one bathroom run for her excited little boy.

Theresa finally got ready for bed herself, put her pajamas on, and wrapped a few more presents in her bedroom, no small chore since she had to fight King off for every piece of wrapping paper. She was exhausted, but she knew she couldn't go to sleep just yet. She crawled into bed, turned off her light, and listened.

Fifteen minutes later, she heard him. Little feet pitter-pattering down the hallway, sneaking toward the living room. King heard him too and jumped up in bed. "Shh," Theresa said to the dog. She petted him and rubbed his tummy, calming the little puppy. Next she heard the gentle clinking of a few dishes, a chair being moved on the kitchen floor, and the refrigerator door opening and closing. Theresa smiled to herself as she continued to soothe King. A few minutes later, the pitter-patter occurred again, this time ending in Tiger's bedroom.

Theresa switched the light back on and waited another fifteen minutes, reading to pass the time. Then she shut King in the bedroom and tiptoed down the hall to Tiger's room. He was now sleeping, his mouth wide-open as he lay sprawled across the bed.

She padded through the kitchen and into the cramped living room. She found the plate that Tiger had just prepared, with two Christmas cookies and a napkin on it and a glass of milk sitting next to it. There was also a note that said *For Santa*, written on the white paper with wide blue lines that Tiger used to make sure his capital letters were just the right height.

Theresa smiled, proud of her son's careful penmanship. She ate most of the cookies, leaving only a few bites. After drinking the milk, she wrote a quick note of thanks on the paper, telling Tiger and Hannah what good kids they were, reminding them to obey their parents. She knew that technically the kids weren't supposed to believe in Santa, but this had been her and Tiger's routine the past two years, and she really didn't see any harm in it. She burped—Santa Claus couldn't have done it better—then headed back to bed.

She turned off the light, pulled the blankets up to her chin, and listened to the cold wind howling outside. She closed her eyes and started in on her prayers, thanking God for sending His Son as a babe in a manger. She thanked God for the warm bed and her food for the day and the fact that she had made it to Christmas without going completely broke. She prayed for Thomas and her pastor and the president and missionaries. She prayed until her thoughts became jumbled so badly that she wasn't sure even God could figure them out. And then she quietly drifted to sleep before she could say "Amen," content in the knowledge that when she awoke it would be Christmas and that soon Thomas would be coming home, the greatest Christmas gift of all . . .

She hadn't been asleep long when she began to dream that she still had all her Christmas shopping to do on Christmas Eve and she couldn't find Thomas, despite searching frantically. Then she was back home, trying to wrap presents for the kids, when she heard a voice outside. King heard it too and let out a throaty little growl.

At first she was scared, but she was drawn like one of her children to the Christmas tree. She practically floated through the kitchen, flicking on the light as she went, then into the living room, where . . . there he was! Thomas! Standing in the middle of the room, big as life. Bigger. Dressed like Santa! Heavier than the last time Theresa had seen him . . . and with a long white beard . . . but it was definitely Thomas. "Theresa," he said. "Theresa, it's me."

For a moment she stood there frozen by the shock of seeing Thomas next to the fireplace and the presents under their Charlie Brown tree, but this one was as tall as the tree in Rockefeller Center. She rushed toward him, embraced him, felt the whiskers on her cheek. He kissed her, then licked her on the cheek.

"Theresa," he said softly, holding her arm. "I'm home."

"Mmm." She closed her eyes to kiss him, then . . . wait, he had licked her? A fireplace? Their trailer had no fireplace!

She opened her sleepy eyes, and he was leaning over the bed, shaking her gently, holding her right arm. She shook her head to clear the cobwebs of her dream, then blinked, but he was still there!

"Thomas?"

"I'm home, Theresa."

"Thomas!"

She threw her arms around him, squeezing him for all she was worth. "What are you doing here?" she whispered.

King was jumping and *licking*, jealous of the embrace, making a nuisance of himself.

"It's a long story," Thomas said. "But before I answer that—what in the world is *he* doing here?"

45

CHRISTMAS DAY

The word traveled around Possum like wildfire, slowed only slightly by the inconvenience of gossiping on Christmas morning when the kids were trying to open presents. "Thomas is out!" There were several different versions of what had happened, including a spectacular version that resembled the biblical jailbreak from the book of Acts, but with a strong gust of wind taking the place of the earthquake. By midmorning, however, the television news had confirmed a far less heroic version of events. To some, it was downright disappointing.

Thomas had signed a promise not to set up his manger scene (or any manger scene) in the Possum town square.

Judge Cynthia Baker-Kline had won.

About 10:00 a.m., local stations began reporting that Judge Baker-Kline had visited the jail late on Christmas Eve and talked with Thomas for nearly an hour. It was a private meeting, and nobody knew the details, but afterward Thomas signed a document saying he would behave himself and not erect any manger scenes on public property. The judge immediately lifted the contempt order and, according to reliable inside sources, even went so far as to give Thomas Hammond a ride home.

It was bad enough that the Possum town hero had folded at the eleventh hour, but then the news started circulating that the judge had the audacity to call a press conference to rub it in. She scheduled it for two in the afternoon at her house, and soon the phone lines in Possum were buzzing with a plot for a hastily called protest. It was Christmas Day, usually a slow news day, so the national spotlight would be focused on Judge Baker-Kline. In a show of solidarity, hundreds of Possumites vowed to drive to the judge's property and take part in a somewhat-organized demonstration. The townspeople all decided to meet in the parking lot at Freewill Baptist Church at 1:00 and drive to the judge's house together. They would make their own signs—no four-letter words allowed—and would sing old-fashioned Christmas carols at the top of their lungs, drowning out any efforts by the judge to take credit for another national step down the slippery slope toward paganism.

By 1:30, more than two hundred Possum vehicles (mostly four-wheel drives) and at least a dozen satellite trucks were waiting outside the gates to the judge's driveway, held back by federal marshals until the judge was ready to start her show. The weather couldn't have been better—one of those brisk winter days where the air seemed particularly pure. There were a few wispy clouds high in the sky, but it was mostly sunny and the high was predicted to reach fifty. Pete Winkle circulated past every SUV to collect signatures for his Impeach the Judge petition and to wish folks a merry Christmas.

★

At precisely 2:00 p.m., the marshals let the first vehicles through, and the long line of SUVs started down the judge's driveway. Thomas was already in place, waiting for them. He had great fun watching the stunned looks on the faces of his fellow Possumites as they rounded the corner and caught their first glimpse of the scene before them. Instead of turning into a raucous crowd, shouting and singing, they quietly parked their vehicles all along the length of the driveway and disembarked solemnly, forming a long line in front of Thomas.

Since many of the townsfolk had been first in line, it took several minutes for the first satellite trucks and news vans to break through. When they did, all of the parking spots on both sides of the driveway had already been taken, so they simply parked in the middle of the drive, creating a traffic jam that would undoubtedly take hours to unsnarl. They didn't care—the biggest story of the season was unfolding before them in living color.

There, in the front yard of the elaborate estate of Judge Cynthia Baker-Kline, flanked on each side by a huge and majestic elm tree, was the humble plywood manger scene of

Thomas Hammond, with the line of worshipers growing by the minute. Bebo, as always, was the center of attention. The plywood lamb and ox were holding up quite well, though the ox had to be propped up with some boxes behind it since its stand was broken. The shepherd's staff had been reinforced with a fresh layer of duct tape and now seemed to be pretty sturdy. And, of course, the manger itself had been rebuilt, complete with hay overflowing the top.

Unlike prior manger scenes, this one came complete with an enthusiastic brown and white cocker spaniel named Ollie running from person to person, wagging his tail and greeting everybody in sight while a miniature copy of the dog strained against his leash and barked. Hannah tried her best to calm King but eventually realized it was a lost cause.

The camera crews rushed to get in place, and reporters hustled to the front of the line and started shouting questions.

"Mr. Hammond, is it true you signed an order prohibiting you from setting this manger scene up in the Possum town square?"

"What made you change your mind last night?"

"Is this part of a deal you worked out with the judge?"

It gave Thomas great satisfaction to ignore the reporters. He looked off to his right and exchanged a knowing glance with Theresa. She had the sweetest smile on her face, an expression that reflected his own thoughts. *This is what Christmas is all about.*

Thomas turned a little farther and caught a glimpse of Jasmine and her family. The aspiring lawyer winked, and Thomas nodded, then turned back to the crowd.

"Judge, what's the point of this display?"

"Do you have a statement for the record?"

It was obvious to Thomas that the reporters were wasting their breath, and they soon figured that out as well. The judge was busy. Thomas took a half step to his left, a little closer to the judge, and she glanced at him. As if embarrassed by this split second of eye contact, they both glanced down at the center of attention—the swaddled baby doll in the judge's arms.

In Thomas's humble opinion, Theresa had made a better—at least a much better looking—Virgin Mary than the judge did. But he had to admit, the symbolism was pretty powerful.

The line before them now stretched well down the judge's driveway as people came forward one at a time or in small family groups to stand solemnly before the baby or gently touch the doll's grubby little cheeks. Cameras flashed and whirred, but the talking was subdued, as if the judge's front lawn had somehow been transformed into a cathedral. The first time that somebody knelt, Thomas watched the bewildered expression on the judge's face as she stood there, uncertain what to do.

Thomas moved closer as the kneelers rose and headed back to their cars. "It's a strange feeling, isn't it, Your Honor?" he asked softly.

"I wanted to tell them to stand up," the judge whispered. "But I sensed that I shouldn't. Who am I to tell them how to worship?"

Though Thomas felt the statement was strangely ironic, he knew that this was not the time to bring it up.

The songs started somewhere in the middle of the line, a family or two singing softly, and the voices spread like falling dominoes. One song would finish and another would spontaneously start—"O Come, All Ye Faithful," "O Little Town of Bethlehem," "It Came Upon a Midnight Clear."

After ten or fifteen minutes of this, people singing, shuffling forward, touching the Christ child, telling the judge and Thomas thanks, the judge did something that gave Thomas chills—goose bumps up and down both arms. Though it wasn't part of the plan, and nobody had even suggested it, she walked forward and tenderly knelt beside the manger, placing Bebo in the middle of the straw. Then, instead of rising to rejoin Thomas, she stayed on her knees and bowed her head.

Thomas stood flabbergasted by the sight, so stunned he couldn't move for several seconds. He glanced at Theresa again and saw the tears welling in her eyes. Scripture flashed through his mind—*"At the name of Jesus every knee should bow."* Instinctively he walked next to the judge and took a knee himself, bowing his head too. He placed his hand gently on her shoulder.

Kneeling there together, they worshiped.

Author's Note

FICTION AUTHORS LOVE this section the way lawyers love disclaimers. We get to remind readers that we've made up most of this and that's why the book is *fiction*. There is no Possum, Virginia. There is no Judge Cynthia Baker-Kline or Jazz Woodfaulk or Tiger Hammond. As for Santa Claus . . . well, you make the call on that one.

One thing I don't make up is the law. I try to be accurate on the substantive issues and legal proceedings. There is enough conflict and drama and majesty in our legal system that you don't have to go beyond what's there to write a good story. One particularly thorny issue we confront is the right of citizens to acknowledge God and religious traditions in the public square. I've got an opinion or two on this, but I also know there are good people on both sides of the debate. I've tried to reflect that in this book.

I've also tried my best to do justice to the spirit of my favorite holiday. In all of history, no event is more worthy of our meditation and best storytelling efforts than this: "The Word became flesh and dwelt among us." You'll be the judge of whether I succeeded.

ALSO BY RANDY SINGER

Fiction

Directed Verdict

Irreparable Harm

Dying Declaration

Self Incrimination

The Judge Who Stole Christmas

The Cross Examination of Oliver Finney

False Witness

By Reason of Insanity

The Justice Game

Fatal Convictions

Nonfiction

Live Your Passion, Tell Your Story, Change Your World

Made to Count

The Cross Examination of Jesus Christ

www.randysinger.net

CP0232